THE TEACHER

(SURFER TOWN II)

REBECCA CASTLE

PROLOGUE

LOVE CAN MAKE *you do the strangest things.*

It can make you swoon, it can make you laugh, it can make you cry.

It can even make your heart stop.

But love is rare.

And finding it - true, everlasting love - can sometimes take a lifetime. Once you've had it, you should never let it go, believe me.

I did. I let it go.

A long time ago.

But now I've had the chance to see it again, that rare thing called love. I got to see it work its magic on my brother and my best friend.

Their wedding was when I saw love again.

1

SANDY

IT ALL STARTED the day of the wedding of my brother and my best friend, that day when I saw him again.

Him.

That man, the man of my dreams and of my nightmares, the same man who I'd thought, and *wanted,* never to see again.

Him.

At the wedding.

After all these years.

No, this can't be real. He can't be here.

Everything changed the day that man strolled right on in, right back into my life, acting as if nothing had happened, as if he hadn't broken my heart all those years ago and left it scattered on the ground behind him. Discarded.

Torn apart.

Left behind.

Yeah, that man. The man I never wanted to even think about.

He was back.

Everything changed that wedding day when I saw him again.

* * *

"SANDY, help. There's a problem with the bride. It's an emergency."

The tone of the bridesmaid's voice is already enough to send me on edge, but her franticly delivered words make my heart go into overdrive.

Oh, shit. Here we go.

My hand's already freezing up on the bottle of champagne I've only just pulled from the hotel fridge. It is *very* cold, but I don't have time to freak out over the temperature.

There's an emergency with the bride.

And I am the one to fix it.

"What's happened? What's wrong?" I ask her.

I don't even have to judge the severity of the problem; the bridesmaid's face matches the dark red color of her dress enough to make me immediately understand that this is a CODE RED situation. The kind of situation you need the Maid of Honor for, the kind of situation that calls for the bride's best friend and best friend only.

Other bridesmaids be damned.

It's a real WEDDING DAY EMERGENCY, and I'm now thrust into the middle of it.

All I do is disappear for one minute to get some chilled champagne and suddenly all hell breaks loose.

Typical. I guess this is the life of a Maid of Honor on her best friend's wedding day. It's what I've signed up for.

"There's no time to explain," the tomato-colored brides-maid - I think her name is Tiffany - splutters at me from the doorway of the hotel room. "We need to go to her. Now."

The last and only time I met this particular bridesmaid, at the hen party, I was in a pretty intoxicated state. I currently don't have the full confidence, or enough memory of our first meeting, to definitively call her Tiffany. Instead, I nod my head at her like a military commander and follow maybe-Tiffany out of the room and into the hotel hallway, bringing along the freezing cold champagne bottle with me. I have a feeling that this emergency situation potentially requires the medicinal properties of bubbly wine.

And I'm not wrong.

We burst into the suite at the end of the hotel hallway, and a horrific scene presents itself to us. A whole gaggle of bridesmaids surround the bride, fanning and fussing around her like a pack of chickens. I don't know any of them - don't even get me started on how *messy* the hen party was. They're all American friends of the American bride, flown into Australia for the hen party and for today. Their loud voices and American accents flood the room in a cacophony of noise. I can't even see the bride through the sea of dresses flapping around like waves, but I can pick out she's sitting down on the hotel floor, her white dress spraying around her on the carpet.

It's worse than a scene out of a Vietnam war movie.

A bloodbath.

I know instantly that it's my responsibility, as Maid of Honor and, more importantly, best friend of the bride, to take full control of the situation and to restore order to the wedding universe. I take in a deep breath and shout.

"Everybody, out!"

The whole room falls silent. All eyes turn to me. I am

unmoved. They need to go. I know another lungful of air and another shout is needed.

"Now!"

They shuffle out of the room. Recognizing the chain of command means that I am the one with all the power.

Good.

I'm treating this like a full-blown military operation. Forget a Vietnam war movie; this is my best friend's wedding. It's more intricate and delicate than planning the Allied invasion of France.

The room fully clears of the swarm of American bridesmaids, meaning I can finally breathe again. Relief.

Now to fix this problem.

I carefully walk over to the bride and sit on the hotel floor next to her, placing the bottle of champagne next to me like it's my most prized possession. I turn to the deflated bride and smile.

"Hey, Ripley. Now, what's wrong?" I ask. "Why have you gotten all those bridesmaids' knickers in a twist?"

My best friend, Ripley, looks back at me with her big doe eyes. Her wavy brown hair falls perfectly on her shoulders. Her pale skin glows, even in the hotel's trashy lighting. God, she's so beautiful. I can see why my younger brother fell in love with her. "I'm just so confused, Sandy," she says softly to me.

"What about?"

"This." She gestures around at the hotel suite. The place is a mess. Glasses, makeup, bags lay scattered around like it's a bombsite. I take it all in.

Yeah, what was I saying about Vietnam?

"Everyone has doubts on their wedding day," I say, trying to avoid looking at the mess around us for too long.

Ripley seems unconvinced. "Yeah?"

"Come on, it's like the *biggest* cliché to have second

thoughts on the day you fully commit to another person. Of course, you have doubts," I reply. "It's only natural."

"It is?"

"Yeah. But you, of all people, shouldn't. You know why?"

"Why?" She's hanging off my every word now. I know this is the most important moment of my short Maid of Honor career. A lot is at stake here.

This is what I was signed up to do. I'm reliable old Sandy, here to calm down another war zone.

"Because you and my stupid brother have found love, that's why."

"Yeah?"

"Do you even know how rare love is? How so many people go through life never finding it? But you've found it. I watched it grow between you and Cove. I watched you two together for the last year. You two have found the rarest and most powerful thing, Ripley, and you should never let it go. I should know, I had it once and it was taken from me, so I'm a bit of an expert when it comes to finding and losing love and what I see with you and Cove is one hundred percent verified, true real love. One hundred percent. Undeniable. True love. Okay?"

"Okay."

"I mean, God, look at you both," I playfully punch Ripley on her arm. "You know, it's absolutely *sickening* seeing my younger brother so infatuated."

"We *are* pretty infatuated."

"I honestly don't know what you see in him, but what I do see is love between you two. The best kind of love. Don't let it go just because you're reverted back to your American ways with all your hometown friends being here and are being super over-emotional."

Ripley laughs, and I see color rush back into her adorable cheeks. It's good to see her laugh again.

The American bridesmaids are clearly listening at the door because once Ripley laughs, they all come tumbling back into the suite like a swarm of ants discovering a lump of sugar and I know my job here is done. I've restored peace and stability back to the wedding universe.

Ripley ignores her childhood friends and pinches my cheek, still laughing. I let her play lovingly with my face this one time, seeing as it's her wedding day and all. "You," she says to me with a twinkle in her eye. "You, Sandy, are the best friend anyone could have. You're so selfless and amazing and giving."

"Stop it," I warn. I don't like this sincere and mawkish sentimentality. "Please don't get all American on me."

"I know it's your cute Aussie nature not to let me compliment you, but please," she says. "It's my wedding day and I get to do what I want to. You are just the most generous and funny soul."

"Stop it."

"Honestly, what would I do without you, Sandy? You brought me here to this country and let me fall in love with your brother without even a single angry word spoken. You work as a teacher to genuinely help kids when you could've done anything you wanted in the world. You've organized the drunkest and messiest hen party in the whole of wedding history."

"That's my natural skill."

"And you know the exact words to cheer me up on the darkest moment of doubt on my wedding day. You're my best friend, Sandy."

She hugs me then. A tight, deep embrace and I don't have the words to properly reply to what she's said to me, despite my remarks. It's just too much. This is just too much. I'm on the verge of actually *crying*, and I never cry.

Great, now I'm getting the American sentimentality virus.

All the power I have left in me is to hug her back and whisper, "thank you."

And I mean it.

"And don't you ever doubt it for a second, Sandy, but you *will* find love one day. I know you think it's rare, but you'll find it. For sure."

I shake my head weakly. "I don't think I'll find love again, not after what happened to me."

"I'm sure you will."

"Men really do like to cheat, don't they? They're all bastards, the fuckers."

One of the bridesmaids turns her head to me with a horrified expression on her face. I think that one's actually Tiffany. Her mouth hangs open at my comment. I guess she doesn't like my swearing.

Ripley, sensing what's up, turns to her and shrugs. "It's one of Sandy's jokes," she explains. Judging from her face, I don't think the bridesmaid fully understands humor. Or Australians.

It's one of my jokes but, deep down, I know it's true. I don't think I'd find love again. Not after what'd happened to me all those years ago.

I'm content with that, though. *Really*, I am. I don't need a man. I don't need love.

"How about we pop open this bubbly?" I suggest, wiping away the beginnings of tears from my eyes as I raise the freezing cold bottle of champagne above my head. The whole room erupts in enthusiastic agreement. It seems like a woman's love of champagne exceeds the borders of both Australia and America.

It's going to be a good wedding.

* * *

AND IT IS.

Cove and Ripley have gotten married on the beach. It suits them perfectly to a T. They fell in love over surfing, so it's only right they get a wedding on the sand with the waves crashing to the side.

Cove's my younger brother. A pro surfer. He suffered a life-changing accident two years ago when he fell off his board during an important surfing competition. It was so bad he required surgery on his legs. His supermodel girl-friend quickly broke up with him and all his surfing contracts dried up overnight. He emerged from hospital months later a broken man. He turned to drinks and drugs and lots, and I mean *lots*, of girls to cope. He refused to surf again, to even touch a surfboard again. My Dad and I tried everything to get him out of his deadly spiral, but nothing worked. He either slept with or verbally abused every psychiatrist in the Southern Hemisphere. Nothing worked at all; we were at the end of our tether.

And then along came Ripley.

My best friend from America. We met online, deep on the internet forums of the superhero film series, *The Vindicator Team*. Yeah, a superhero franchise. Silly, I know. But we both *loved* the films and, being the only two females on the internet forums, we bonded pretty damn quickly. Despite me being slightly older and from the other side of the world. Despite her working-class upbringing in Queens, New York, and my completely opposite affluent upbringing as the daughter of a billionaire businessman in the sleepy coastal town of New Water, Australia. We just fit together like pieces of a puzzle. In the months before we met at New Water Airport, we would chat together every day online.

And that's when I came up with the idea of flying Ripley to Australia, to have her stay, rent-free and all-expenses-paid, at my house so that she might be able to help Cove in some way to get back on his feet and on a board again. She wasn't someone Cove knew, so he wouldn't feel ashamed of her knowledge, and she was able to be discreet about our wealthy family and our dark secrets, so I trusted her. She was our last hope in reforming Cove. Dad agreed to the plan, and soon Ripley was flying out to Australia.

And she did a lot more than reform Covethe Cove. It was a bit tricky at first, but they both actually fell in love.

Which led to this day on the beach. This beautiful day with the sun shining down and the water blue and clear.

The day they get married on this beach in front of their family and friends.

It's just amazing, and it's even romantic enough to touch my cold, dead heart.

The look on Cove's face when he saw how beautiful and radiant Ripley looked in her wedding dress would make any bitter older sister melt, including me. The way he smiles at her; that's proper, heartwarming stuff Hollywood could never fully replicate.

The wedding's perfect in every way.

And then it's the afterparty. Back at the hotel.

This is the time for this Maid of Honor to let her hair down and party. I've been looking forward to this part the most when I can finally dance gawkily with Ripley and seriously sing my heart out to the *Grease* soundtrack medley all night long and not have to worry about another WEDDING DAY EMERGENCY.

But none of that fun stuff is meant to be.

Oh, no.

It's only just after I arrive at the hotel conference room, now decked out for the party, that I see him.

Him.

Skipper. Skipper Deep.

Skipper *fucking* Deep.

The man from my nightmares I never want to see again. He's here.

It all happens so quickly. I see him across the hotel conference room. He sees me.

And then, before I can even react, he starts walking quickly in one direction.

I know where he's going, but I don't have time to react or to get away.

He's heading in one direction. He's heading straight for me.

2

SKIPPER

THERE SHE IS.

Sandy Finn.

She's right there, standing just across the room from me. She's staring at me with those irresistible light blue eyes of hers, looking like she hasn't aged a day since I last saw her eight years ago.

Eight long years ago.

It's definitely Sandy Finn. She hasn't changed at all, not one bit since the last time I saw her.

And now, there she is, not that far away from me across the hotel conference room, and she's staring at me.

She's spotted me, and I, *for sure*, have spotted her.

I take a step forward towards her, and then another, and then another.

I knew I'd find her here.

Her brother's wedding.

Of course, she'd have to be here. It was too easy.

I have to admit, I've been *pretty* nervous about seeing

her again. Even last night, sitting in my private jet flying over from Los Angeles to New Water, I couldn't still my restless head. She tumbled through my thoughts as reliably as the sun rising every morning. Thoughts about what would happen when we meet again have haunted my dreams every night since I received the wedding invitation, and her face has haunted me the entire flight over from America. I haven't even been able to sleep properly the whole of last week like I've been some giddy schoolgirl anxiously waiting for prom. I've actually been *nervous* about meeting her again.

And I never get nervous.

But the possibility of seeing Sandy Finn again has made me act so *unnatural*, so unlike my usual self. Eight years later and she still has that power over me, that power to make me go weak at the knees with a single word. That power to devastate my soul with just one glance.

The same glance she's giving me right here, in this conference room, as I walk towards her.

It only makes me want her more.

Oh, that I do. I want her so much.

When I got the invitation to Cove's wedding in the post, I was shocked at first. Sitting there, in my high-rise luxury apartment in Los Angeles, I'd thought that Cove Finn had made a mistake in sending me an invite to his wedding happening all the way over in New Water. But he hadn't.

It was no mistake. I've been invited on behalf of Cove and Sandy's father, Michael Finn. Owner of Finn Companies. My own family's company had many business dealings with them right back to before I was born, and I have closely dealt with the American side of the Finn business empire since I've moved to America a year ago.

Of course, Sandy would never have known that. I know she would've freaked out if she saw that her dad and his business had invited me to her brother's wedding. She's never wanted any part of her father's business, never taken any interest in it. Instead, she's become a teacher or something; that was the last thing I've heard. And, of course, Michael Finn didn't know what had gone down between Sandy and me eight years ago when he sent me that wedding invitation in the post. He probably thought of me as one of the family's friends, someone who'd also grown up in New Water along with Cove and Sandy. A prominent locally-born-and-bred businessman who should be invited to the wedding of the town's most famous surfer.

Nobody out of the ordinary at all to Michael Finn.

So, it wasn't exactly *unusual* to get a wedding invitation. And, normally, when it came to weddings, I tend to skip them without a second's thought. I don't have time for drinking and partying or the awful sentimentality that traditionally comes with the ceremony. No, not for me. Not for Skipper Deep.

But the prospect of seeing Sandy again spiked my curiosity. I replied positively to the wedding invitation without even thinking about it. And now, a few months later, here I am, back in my old hometown after eight long years walking across the room towards Sandy Finn.

The twists and turns of life.

All the money I have, all the high-end properties I own around the world, all the business deals I've made, and all the staff that work for me in 5 different time zones. All of that means nothing when it comes to Sandy Finn. Eight years later and she still has control over my dreams and my heart. No amount of money can solve a problem like Sandy Finn. I knew the only thing I had to do when I received that invitation in the post, the only way to still my restless mind, was to fly back to New Water and see her again. I knew the wedding of her brother was my chance, the one time I knew where she'd be for certain.

The one time she would have to speak to me.

I'm determined to reach her in this conference room, reach her before she disappears on me. I'm determined to speak to her. I know she'll want to get away from me, but she can't leave the afterparty of her brother's wedding. She just *has* to talk to me here. The room isn't even crowded; people are still making their way back from the beach, so the place is quiet. They slowly stream in one by one.

Perfect conditions for me to speak to her.

But I knew Sandy would be here early, just as she always is. She's always the early bird, ready to solve any potential disaster that's looming. Oh, I know her like the back of my hand. We know each other so well. Eight years apart won't change the depth of mutual understanding we have between us.

She has to speak to me now. She's trapped.

It's been strange being back in New Water after all this time. The last I saw of the town was the last time I ever saw Sandy. The last time I was even in Australia. All these familiar streets of my childhood are just the same. Nothing has changed. The same buildings I remember stand on every corner. The places. The beach. It's still the sleepy coastal town that dominates my memories. Nothing has changed, just like Sandy. I recognize a lot of faces at the wedding. Small towns are like that. It's been a blast from the past.

But I'm not here for the trip down memory lane. No. I'm here for one thing, and one thing only.

Sandy Finn.

The last person I ever saw when I left New Water eight years ago was her. And now I'm back in town, and all I want to do is see her again.

I wave to my bodyguard, Steve, to not follow me as I walk across that hotel conference room right up to her.

The girl from my memories.

She stands there with a shocked expression that turns into disgust and anger as I approach. Just as I know she would, just as I expect, but I am not deterred. This is what I've dreamed about every night since I got the wedding invitation. Sandy Finn has haunted all my sleeping hours for the past few months, and I need to resolve this.

The girl from my dreams.

Even up close, she still looks the same as she did when we were teenagers. Tall, slim, with long wavy blonde hair and her Aussie tanned skin. Nothing has changed about her at all. She'd blossomed young and had stayed beautiful, just like she had been in my dreams. But she is even better than my dreams.

She is real.

And she's now standing in front of me. I walk up to her and smile my best smile.

"Hi," I say, and from her response I know shit's about to go down.

3

SANDY

His stupid smile.

His stupid, *gorgeous* smile.

I thought I'll never see that smile again, not in a million years. My body goes weak at the sight of him and I know right there that he's going to undo me.

No, Sandy. Don't you dare fall for one of his stupid tricks.

"Hi," he says when he reaches me. I have nowhere to run, nowhere to escape from Skipper Deep. All the time it takes for him to stroll his cocky little walk across the room to me, I do absolutely nothing.

I don't run.

I don't flee.

Instead, I stay frozen to the spot, shocked at seeing his face again after all these years apart. He knows he'd shock me here. This has been his evil plan, knowing I can't escape from this place. He knows he can talk to me in this conference room at the wedding of my brother, and I have no way of running away.

Hi.

With his single word of greeting, he's stripped me utterly bare. All the defenses I've built up over the last eight years fall apart at his first word. Tattered. Ruined. My defenses are no help to me now. I can do nothing against him or his power over me. This is the worst thing; the knowledge that one word from him can still transform me back into that weak, blubbering teenage girl I thought I've exterminated inside me. Eight years later and he still has a supernatural power over me and my heart.

Plus, he still looks *devastatingly* handsome. That doesn't help at all.

He wears an expensive black suit that barely conceals how athletic his muscular body is. His stubble is immaculately kept like an elite soccer player. His brown eyes sparkle. His jawline is made by the gods. His short brown hair's thick with years of careful, and probably *very* expensive, management. He's utterly exquisite in every way, just as he'd been when we were teenagers. Charming and alluring. Like fine wine. Vintage. That's Skipper Deep summed up.

I just simply can't take my eyes off him.

I shake my head, recovering from the initial shock of seeing him again, from the initial shock of seeing a real-life *ghost* appear at my brother's wedding.

"What the hell are you doing here?" I ask him, stuttering over the words as I try, and fail, to remain composed.

Be strong, Sandy. Don't show him weakness. He'll pounce at the first sign of trouble.

He continues smiling his awful, gorgeous smile at me. "I was invited, of course."

"What?"

"By your dad," he replies. "He invited me here. It was a shock to see the invitation in the post, but I thought why not? Why not take the chance and visit my hometown? See some old friends like you."

Old friends? Me? Not after what you did, buddy.

I try to be firm. Unwavering. I'm putting my metaphorical foot down now before this gets out of hand. "You should not be here," I say, straightening my shoulders. I try not to be intoxicated by his mesmerizing appearance. All my old desires resurface just by looking at him; all those old teenage feelings I thought I've locked away forever are flooding back into my body, hardening things. Making me wet. Making this impossible.

"Your dad invited me here, though. And I think I deserve a bit more courtesy from you, Sandy."

Courtesy?

I throw my arms up in pure anger. "Tell me one thing before I throw you out of here, Skipper."

"Ouch. You're vicious."

"Tell me one thing. The last words I ever said to you, do you remember them?"

"Of course," Skipper replies. He doesn't appear fazed by me or my aggressiveness. He isn't fazed by much, never has been. It's so infuriating, but so mesmerizing to watch.

"Well, what were they? The last words I said to you last time we saw each other?"

"You said you never wanted to see me again."

"Bingo," I reply, spinning around and marching over to the bar.

That's enough, that should be enough to let him know I don't want to speak to, or even see, him.

But with Skipper Deep it's not that easy. I know him.

He's a lion on the prowl, and he's not going to stop until he has his prey.

Me.

I take one of the prepared filled glasses of champagne ready on the bar and drown it in one without looking back over the shoulder at him. At Skipper Deep. The bubbles tickle my throat as the champagne goes down. I need to do something to quiet my nervous shaking hands.

Just as I expect, Skipper follows me over to the bar. I don't turn around to face him, not even when he approaches and stands right next to me. I can even smell his overwhelming expensive aftershave; that's how close we were. The man is *expensive*. Tailored suit from Saville Row. Elite aftershave. Perfectly cut hair. He's the very definition of a young, successful international bachelor businessman.

Yuck, can he get even more irritating with his beauty?

He's changed a lot in eight years, but he is still gorgeous. He still makes my hands shake with nerves when he looks at me.

"It's been a long time," he says as he leans on the bar, inches away from my body. I pride myself on not giving in to the temptation of looking at him.

"Eight years," I correct.

That's how long it's been since he broke my heart.

"Yeah, a long time, and now I'm back. What do you think about that?"

"Your accent has changed," I say, reaching for another glass of champagne. "You sound British."

He does. There's no trace of his rough teenage Aussie accent left in his voice. It's all replaced by the cut-glass refined accent of a rich and confident English aristocrat.

"When I left here, I went to the UK and spent the last years of education in a posh boarding school. From there I moved to America to take control over my family's business. That's where I've lived ever since," he explains.

I still don't look at him.

"I don't care," I reply.

"Hey, you asked why I sound British, and that's my response."

"So, British boarding school, that's why you sound pretentious. Finally, you sound like your personality," I say with a healthy dose of snark before taking another sip.

Skipper chuckles, inching in closer towards me with his face. "Yeah, maybe that's why," he says. His easy-going cocky attitude infuriates me. I just want to turn around and slap that chiseled face of his. That'll deal with his smarmy behavior and mocking voice. "Still the same old Sandy I see, ready with the right quip and mocking comeback."

"Oh, yes."

"And what have you been up to all these years? I've heard you're a teacher."

"Yep."

Short and sweet. Skipper doesn't take the heavy hint. He remains standing at the bar next to me.

"So, the rumors are true. You're not taking a penny from your father. Instead, you're making your own way in the world. That's pretty commendable, Sandy."

"Screw your compliments. They're not going to work on me this time."

"So, they have worked on you before, back when we were teenagers?"

"They never did."

"Sandy, do you remember those old times? The fun we had together?"

Of course, I remember the fun times. My body will never let me forget them.

"I was young and stupid."

"You seemed to love every moment, if I recall correctly."

"Not every moment."

"Ah, so you *did* love it. Good to know."

"You're not just here for the wedding," I say, changing subjects from my family's wealth and those hot sexual past experiences with Skipper. "Why are you truly here? What's the real reason you've flown back here?"

"I can't just fly back to attend the wedding of a family friend?"

"Not when that family includes me."

"It's good to see you too, Sandy."

I turn to him then. Skipper's still smiling. He always liked to smile a lot. I *hate* it, but at the same time, I truly don't. Not really. Skipper's smile was the reason why I fell in love with him in the first place all those years ago, and he knows it. He knows how his charming smile can destroy me.

And it's destroying my insides now.

"It's been eight years, Skipper. Eight years since you broke my heart. It takes a lot of balls to come to the wedding of my brother and walk back into my life like nothing's happened."

"A lot of balls? So, you *do* remember the old times."

"I remember those times. They were fun. Really, *really* fun."

"You really did love them."

"But you broke my heart and now that you've shown up and embarrassed me just like you wanted, how about you leave?"

"I don't want to embarrass you, Sandy."

"Too late for that."

"Do you want me to apologize for what happened?"

What? Apologize for what happened eight years ago? Forget it.

"I'm over this conversation and I'm over you, Skipper. I want you to go now and never come back," I say.

He tuts. "That's cruel, Sandy."

"Not as cruel as what you did to me."

"How about I buy you a drink?"

"No."

"Have a drink with me, Sandy Finn."

"No."

He clasps his hands together mockingly. *"Please?"* His voice drips with sarcasm. Oh, how I *hate* him despite his overwhelmingly good looks.

"I will never get a drink with you. Not in a million years. Not with any man, and certainly not with you, Skipper Deep."

Without waiting, or *caring*, for his response, I immediately turn around from the bar and walk away in the opposite direction. I carry on walking until I reach the front doors of the conference room. I spot a family friend and immediately rush up to greet her. I need to be doing something, *anything*, to ward Skipper away. To pretend everything's normal. He doesn't follow me this time, and I'm relieved.

I've got him.

I'm proud of myself and for the way I handled that man, that handsome man who thought he can waltz right on back into my life, and who thought we could get drinks together even after what he did to me eight years ago. That gorgeous, confident man who thought he had me cornered at my brother's wedding. I've beaten him. I've rejected him. I've got him.

I gush over the family friend's dress and avoid looking back over at the bar. I avoid looking back at Skipper Deep. I don't want to give the man the satisfaction of knowing I was still thinking about him. I don't want him to know I can't get him, or his delicious face, out of my mind. I continue the conversation with my friend, aware that Skipper's eyes are still focused on me.

It's only when more wedding guests have streamed into

the conference room that I give in to the temptation to check back on Skipper. I just want to see him one more time.

I turn. And there he is, on the other side of the room, still at the bar.

My heart lodges in my throat.

Oh, God.

He's still staring at me. From across the room, he's still staring at me with that gorgeous smirk across his face.

For the second time this evening, my body goes weak at the sight of him.

He truly has stripped me utterly bare.

4

ONE WEEK LATER

SANDY

"Okay guys, who can tell me about what Romeo and Juliet is about?"

Absolute silence greets me as I scan the classroom in front of me, searching for an answer amongst my many students.

Awkward, uncomfortable silence.

"No answer?"

Yep. None.

The group of eleven-year-olds of my English class stare dumbly back at me, their eyes aimless and their attention lacking. Clearly, Romeo and Juliet isn't as catchy as their TikToks and PlayStations. Clearly, their teacher is not as interesting as a streaming gamer on YouTube.

Okay, this is going to be a lot harder than I thought.

Monday. At school. It's the first day of trying to teach a

class full of bored children the intricacies of one of the finest pieces of literature and it's already started off on an awkward footing. Great.

So much for eager minds and all that.

No one raises their hand. No one even seems remotely interested in what I'm saying out here in front of them. This is just another stupid class to them, but to me this is Shakespeare.

Shakespeare.

The finest wordsmith to ever live. The man who made me fall in love with the English language and reading and poetry and plays. I want these kids to feel the same passion I do, to change their lives in the same way mine was changed when I first read the man's work.

I know what I have to do. I've got to juice this up, make it appealing to the Snapchat generation.

Do your thing, Sandy. Be a good teacher.

I take a step forward into the middle of the classroom, just ahead of the whiteboard. All the kids, sitting at their little desks, stare back gormlessly at me.

A captive audience. Literally, they can't leave.

Time to let my inner actress shine.

Let's launch into this. Let's teach them a love of words.

I don't even hesitate.

"But, soft! What light through yonder window breaks? It is the east, and Juliet is the sun."

Nothing. No response to my Oscar-worthy performance. One girl starts doodling in her notebook. The boy next to her starts to rip his up.

Right, fine, I'm no Judi Dench. I can live with that. Maybe.

"No? Okay, let me try another line," I say to my bored onlookers. I lift my arms up dramatically like a melodramatic Shakespearean stage actor, and bellow out the next few lines. "Love is heavy and light, bright and dark, hot and cold, sick and healthy, asleep and awake. It's everything except what it is!"

The loudest applause I get is a cough from someone in the front row. I think it's Nick, he's usually always absent due to some cold. I put his cough down to his allergies and not to a deep understanding of Elizabethan playwrights or an appreciation of my dramatic performance. Everyone else looks like they'd rather be in after-school detention than sitting in here listening to their twenty-five-year-old teacher slowly go crazy over lines written four hundred years ago. And who can blame them?

It's not exactly the life-changing education I thought I'd be giving out as a teacher.

This is hopeless. I'm a terrible teacher. I can't even raise a laugh at my pathetic acting display.

This is the same classroom where I learned to love Shakespeare nearly a decade ago, and now I'm teaching it in the same space. This is the same school I was sent to for my own education.

Poseidon's Academy.

One of the most elite schools in the country. Every student has to wear the special uniform of the Academy. Tie and blazers. I can't believe I get to teach at the same place I used to be a student at. In some ways it's great, in others it's strange. There's a lot of memories in these rooms and hallways.

A lot of memories containing Skipper Deep.

We used to do a lot of steamy stuff in here.

Forget about him. That was a week ago, and you haven't seen him since. He's out of your life, probably gone back to America or hell or wherever hole he crawled out of.

"How about we start slowly and then build-up to the famous lines, hey?" I ask the class rhetorically. Well, I intend it to be rhetorical. No one in this room will answer me, anyway. "How about we run over the story of the play and the basic background of the time it was written in first, shall we?"

Still, no answers.

I've been a teacher for nearly three years and I still feel as lost as my first day when it comes to getting a classroom's attention. I think I'm one of those teachers who takes some time for students to warm up to, but when they do, it's the best moments. That's how it's worked in the past. But, right now, this class is not warmed up; they're more like a frozen bit of chicken. I'm gonna have to really work hard this term to get them up to speed.

Before the big exams.

The scary, job-destroying exams. A measure of my teaching prowess.

Sandy, don't think about the exams. Don't think about your job being on the line.

I turn to the whiteboard and start writing out what scenes the students will have to read by the next class. At this rate, I may have to resort to my nuclear option and put on the film *Romeo + Juliet*. At least Leonardo DiCaprio might be able to teach these kids a line or two of Shakespeare.

I have just started writing out the whole "two households" bit when I hear a commotion behind me. Someone starts yelling. A boy's voice. I turn around quickly to see two of the kids in the back row, Tom and James, full-on fighting each other.

Like real, proper *fighting*.

Jesus.

They're really going at each other. The full Monty. Arms wrapped around the other. Heads butting. Bodies falling to the floor. It only takes a second before the whole class is on their feet, enthusiastically cheering the two boys on. Egging each one to do more damage to the other. The words coming out of Tom and James' mouths are indecipherable, a series of grunts and the occasional swear word. I hadn't heard such filth from a pair of eleven-year-olds before.

This is, for sure, much more attention-grabbing for the class than my little acting display.

I drop my whiteboard marker and storm towards the two fighting boys. The other kids move out of my way.

I don't really know what to do. I've never dealt with a fight like this before.

Do I get physical and rip one boy off the other? Is that even allowed? Will I get sued by an irate parent? What do I do?

What do I do?

"Stop," I say to them, my voice wavering. My lack of confidence is pretty evident.

Not the best start.

"Stop fighting."

Tom and James ignore me. They're too busy engaged with beating the seven hells out of each other to listen to the weak commands of their English teacher.

"Stop it, boys."

No response beyond the continued grunting and swearing.

They're getting even more violent now, thrashing and biting at each other. Tom pulls at James' collar and they tumble towards the classroom door, the other children scrambling to get out of their way. Tom and James don't care about the other students, they are engaged in a battle to the death. They don't care about their collateral damage or their exasperated English teacher franticly following them. Even though they're just young boys, I know that a single punch from one of them can knock me to the ground. I've got to be careful.

The last thing I need on my job-performance card is that I was knocked out by a stray punch of one of my students.

"Stop this right now! Stop fighting!"

Tom pulls at James' shirt until they stumble out of the classroom. They're in the school hallway now, making such a loud noise that students from other classes have streamed out of their own rooms, sensing blood's gonna be spilled any moment. Kids are like sharks, attracted to even the *prospect* of blood. It seems like half the school is fitted into this hallway, forming a spectator circle around the two boys as they duke it out in full view of everyone.

Well, this wasn't how my first class on Romeo and Juliet was meant to go, that's for sure.

I work my way through the gathering crowd of watching students and make it into the makeshift boxing ring. The boys don't pay any attention to me. They've started trading insults at each other.

"You took my phone!" Tom is clearly not happy. He snarls at James, wagging his finger threateningly.

"No, I did not." James shakes his head. He's not exactly pleading with the other boy or explaining himself, instead, he's mocking him.

"Yes, you did."

"I did not."

"Yes, you did. You took my phone. I saw you."

"No, you didn't see me do anything. Why would I want your stupid phone, anyway? It's like five years old."

That's enough for Tom. He lunges at James, smacking him across the face. Now there really is blood. James looks bad. His face is already purple.

I think his nose is bleeding.

James cries out, half in pain and half in tears, and flails his arms towards Tom, who bats him away easily. This is going to launch into total warfare at any moment. It's beyond a gladiatorial contest now.

This is a real fight to the death.

"Stop it, both of you," I cry out in despair. Nobody listens. I'm actually afraid some serious physical damage is going to be dealt out soon if I don't stop this. Then my teaching career would really be over, forget about the exams. I'll be a goner for sure.

"STOP."

The word echoes down the hallway, and everyone stops. But it wasn't me who said it.

We all turn to the source of the voice.

I know who it is even before looking.

Miss Tweed.

The head of the mathematics department, and one of the scariest people I've ever come across.

No wonder everyone's stopped at her command.

She marches down the hallway. Even though she's five feet tall and the shortest person I know, Miss Tweed takes up the hallway of the school like a mythical, all-powerful giant. She really is terrifying. A thing of nightmares. And she's heading straight for Tom, James, and me.

Shit.

I feel sorry for the two boys for what they're in for when Miss Tweed gets involved. I'm scared of her myself and I'm a fellow teacher.

She doesn't say anything else as she marches down the hallway towards us. She doesn't need to. Everyone, and I mean *everyone*, has stopped what they're doing and are looking at her. She's brought half the school to utter silence with just one strong word.

She's supernatural.

She reaches us, standing next to me. She looks down at the two boys with a grimace that, if looks could kill, would burn a hole into their skulls.

I don't know her age, but if I had to guess, it'd be around the early sixties. She's tiny, with huge puffy brown hair that takes up a third of her height. I've never seen her smile lovingly once. She usually uses her smile to patronize and insult others.

And she is using that smile on me now.

"Miss Finn, how about you take the wounded boy to the school nurse?"

She means James. Fighting stopped, I can fully see him now. He really does have a bleeding nose. Tom's blow really hit him hard. Blood streams uncontrolled from his nostril.

"Okay, Miss Tweed." I didn't know what to say.

"And," she continues, turning to Tom. "I'll deal with the other boy."

Tom gulps in fear, and he should. He's in big trouble now.

So much for my first day teaching my favorite piece of literature.

5

SANDY

THE SCHOOL NURSE is like an angel. I've rushed James over to her station by the main office building of the school, fearing the worst. I told him to lift his head back as we practically run across the campus to the nurse's station, his nose dripping blood like a gushing tap. The fight didn't go well for him. I guide James by gripping his shoulders like a car steering wheel, navigating the hallways of the school like I'm driving a vehicle.

But once the nurse gets ahold of him, she produces some cotton wool and some bandages and within minutes, she's stopped the bleeding and has completely patched James up. She really is an angel; she's miraculously fixed James up in no time, despite my terror.

"Is it still hurting?" I ask the boy. He nods.

"Yeah, but not as much as before."

"That's good." His face is still purple. The fight had been so vicious. So violent. Tom has really done some damage, but at least it just looks superficial. Mostly bruises. And at least his nose has stopped bleeding.

We sit in the nurse's station, amongst various posters for allergies and CPR routines. The nurse has gone to collect some more bandages and to gather some paperwork to do with the incident. James sits on the bed and I've pulled up a chair.

I lean back into my seat and sigh.

That was close, any longer and the fight would've turned serious. All I wanted to do today was teach some Shakespeare, not get involved in an amateur boxing match between my students.

The door knocks and I turn to face it. It opens. I expect it to be the nurse, but it's Miss Tweed standing at the door. She peeks in like a bird of prey, her big nose like a beak.

"How is he?" she asks in a deadpan tone.

I shrug. "He's going to be okay."

"Good," Miss Tweed replies. Her beady, dark green eyes glare at me. "May I talk to you outside, Miss Finn?"

"Sure."

I smile at James and stand up.

Miss Tweed stands waiting for me outside in the hall-way, her hands clasp together in front of her cardigan. She waits until I close the door to the nurse's station before she speaks, but I get there first.

"Before you tell me anything," I say. "Thank you for helping me back there. That fight was bad, and I was trying to control it. If it wasn't for you, then I guess there would've been a lot more damage than two boys' wounded egos."

Miss Tweed pauses and smiles at me with her patron-izing look. She waits until I finish before she launches into full-on attack mode. "You, *Sandy*, handled that whole situation wrongly, if I must say so myself."

It's venomous. It's like she's spitting at me with her words. Miss Tweed and I have never got on well, despite my best intentions. I've tried being kind to her in the staffroom, always asking her how her day was, trying to chat to her. But it's like Miss Tweed's had it out for me since day one. She's been working here for five years, a few longer than I have, and has fully integrated herself as the matriarch of the school. Even the school principal, Mr. Brown, has seemingly seceded all power to her. It's like she's made herself de facto dictator of the school, the person everyone fears most all the way from the principal down to the youngest student. I still try to be kind and courteous and respectful towards her, but it's *definitely* not reciprocated.

I feel like Miss Tweed hates me.

She's certainly making it clear in the hallway outside the nurse's station.

"It was getting a little bit out of hand, yeah."

"A little bit out of hand?" Miss Tweed's eyes widen in mock disbelief. "That's a very subtle way of putting in. A little bit out of hand? That boy in that room there was nearly knocked out cold by another one of your students."

"Thank God it was stopped, then."

"Stopped by me," Miss Tweed says, shaking her head profusely. She hasn't broken eye contact with me once. She barely blinks. She is a terrifying woman. "I mean, *really*. It was your classroom, Sandy. Your rules. I didn't know you led such an unruly mob."

"Hang on," I reply. I'm not letting her get away with lecturing me so easily. "I don't run a free-for-all class. I was teaching them Shakespeare. Two boys got into a wild fight, that's all. I thank you for stepping in and helping me, but these kinds of fights never usually happen under my watch. What happened today was a freak rarity."

"I should hope so. For your sake."

Wait.

Is she threatening me?

"What's that supposed to mean?"

"Let's just say your job is on the line," Miss Tweed replies. Oh, she knows how to deliver a sentence to the maximum devastating impact. She's clearly enjoying bringing me bad news like this, but I do know that if anyone in the school has the knowledge about anyone getting fired, it's her. And she knows I know that. Fear rises in me as I stare back into her dark eyes. She still hasn't broken eye contact with me since I've stepped into the school hallway, and it's really starting to creep me out.

"How so?"

"Ever since you came into this school," Miss Tweed says. "I have noticed a lack of discipline in the English department. I feel as if the students are lacking passion or guidance." She's the head Math teacher, but I never knew she despised the English department so much.

"And you're putting that all down on me?" I ask.

"Yes," Miss Tweed's bluntness shocks me. I realize now that she really is out to get me. I cross my arms, and she continues her attack. "You're young and you're inexperienced. You can't run a smooth classroom, your students fight and you can't even stop them, and worst of all, I think you got this job because of your father."

That came out quick.

I stammer. *"What?"*

I can't believe what she's just said, what she's just accused me of.

She's really brought my dad into this conversation?

Miss Tweed keeps talking, ignoring me. "I think the only reason you got this job is because of how wealthy your family is. Let's be serious and frank here. Your father's connections are the reason you got here. We all know here that your hiring wasn't based on your skill or talent as a teacher, but on the possibility that your rich father will donate to the school."

I don't even know what to say to this.

"Are you being serious?"

Miss Tweed smiles at me again in her trademark condescending manner. I can't believe what she's actually saying to me right now. She's actually *enjoying* being such a cold-hearted bitch. "Yeah, and we need donations. As you know, the school is in dire financial straits. Your father can help with that, no?"

I really can't believe what's she's saying. She's insulting me right here in the school hallway and I'm at a complete loss for words. Yeah, my family is rich, but that's not why I got hired. I worked my ass off to be here, to be qualified as a teacher, and I've strictly forbidden my dad to be involved in any way with my career from day one. I am gob smacked at Miss Tweed's allegations. I can't even reply to what she's saying. I feel small, and Miss Tweed seems giant. She's crushing me like an insect.

She's got me under her little foot.

"Speaking of money and your connections," Miss Tweed continues with her infuriatingly fake sing-song voice. "You better be there at the fundraiser tonight. We need you to schmooze with the rich beneficiaries of the school community. You know how to talk to them. We need you at the fundraiser to do the one job you can do and raise the right money for the school. And being as I am the school's bookkeeper, and the teacher here with the best average results, I must warn you in an official capacity that you need to be on your best behavior tonight. Unlike the behavior of your students we've seen today."

"What?"

"Just remember, I've got my eye on you, Miss Finn. I'm always watching you."

I'm still completely at a loss for words. I can't believe her. I can't believe she's insulting me like this. She really does hate me. She really does think I'm a pathetic teacher. Do all the other staff think the same? Have I been living under the delusion that I was a good teacher all this time? Does everyone at the school despise me the way Miss Tweed does? My head's racing.

Do they all think I've got this job because of who my dad is?

"Thank you, Sandy," she says with that high-pitched tone of hers before she spins around and disappears out the door.

I'm left in the hallway outside the nurse's station, shaking.

It's like Miss Tweed has torn me in shreds. I don't know what to do with myself.

I run to the nearest bathroom, thank God there's nobody in there, and I break down. I lean over the bathroom sink as tears gush out. I *hate* crying. I really do. I try to avoid it. But, right now, I can't. The words that Miss Tweed said to me sting like bullets.

I didn't get this teaching job because of my dad's money or connections. I fought like hell to get here. This was my achievement. But, outside in that hallway, Miss Tweed's gone and thrown it back in my face.

I feel so alone.

So alone in this school. I've tried my hardest to blend in here. To really get integrated with the students and the other teachers, but Miss Tweed's come along to kick me to the curb. I really thought I was a part of this school, but that teacher has thrown my dreams away. All I wanted to do was make friends here and be the best teacher I can be, but Miss Tweed has stamped all over that.

I look at myself in the bathroom mirror. I'm a mess.

I pull out my phone and I dial in Ripley's number. My best friend. I want to talk to her. I want to hear her calming voice. I want to know everything's alright.

It rings a few times before Ripley answers it.

"Hey, Sandy, how're things?"

"Hey. I'm all good," I say. My voice breaks when I hear her voice.

But I'm not good. Not good at all.

"What's the reason for the call?"

"Uh, nothing," I stammer.

"You okay?" Ripley asks. "You sound upset. Is everything alright?"

"Uh, everything's fine."

She waits a moment. It's obvious from my voice that everything is not fine. She knows me too well.

"You don't sound like it is."

"No, everything's fine. I'm just having a moment."

There's a pause on the other end as Ripley thinks. She's trying to judge how upset I really am, and I'm really trying to hide it. "Hey, I can come over tonight if you want," she says. "We can have a girls' night in."

Ripley and Cove used to live at my house until they were engaged. Now they have their own place by the ocean, within walking distance of the beach, where Cove can easily surf every day. Ripley works as a nurse at New Water Hospital. They have a great life, it seems.

I really miss them staying at my place.

Now I'm all alone.

"No," I reply. "Don't worry about coming over tonight. I'm fine. I'm busy tonight anyway with a school fundraiser."

"Another one? Geez, how many does that school need?"

I chuckle. "A lot."

"You sure I can't do anything?"

"I'm sure. I just want to hear your voice, that's all."

We say our goodbyes and hang up. I shake my head and look at myself in the mirror, wiping away the tears from my face.

Miss Tweed's right. All I'm good for is to talk to rich people and raise money for the school.

I'm not a teacher, I'm nothing but a fraud.

6

SANDY

"Okay, time to do this," I say to myself as I open the car door and step outside.

Despite my reassuring words to myself, I don't feel confident, not at all.

Miss Tweed's attack on me outside the nurse's station has really rattled me all day long. Ever since that little confrontation, it's like the ground constantly shifts under my feet. I feel wounded, like a hunted animal, and Miss Tweed's the hunter.

She's out to get me.

I'm in the parking lot of New Water's most pricey hotel, the same hotel my brother and my best friend got married in a week ago, but this time I'm not here for a nice wedding. I'm here for the school fundraiser.

Great.

Men in suits and local celebrities, bad canapes and Miss Tweed.

My favorite way to spend an evening.

Despite being one of the most elite private schools in the country, Poseidon's Academy has fallen on hard financial times in the past few years. I don't know how we have, since we charge extortionate fees for the students to attend the school, but that's what I've been told is the case by both Miss Tweed and the principal. The school is in trouble. Deep trouble. That's why we've been holding fundraisers for the past few months, to try to encourage the rich parents of students and local business people to invest and donate to our school.

This is just the latest one. All run by Miss Tweed, of course. She's made herself in charge of the school's financial records when she came in five years ago. These fundraisers have been her baby, and she runs a tight ship.

And she's just ruined my day.

I know I shouldn't be so down by what she said to me at school earlier, but it has affected me so badly. I'm still recovering from her words in that hallway outside the nurse's station. It's like she's stripped away all my self-confidence and left me with nothing.

You're only here because of your family's wealth and connections.

Lies. What she said simply wasn't true. But somehow Miss Tweed could make me feel like a chastised schoolgirl. She made it seem like she was my teacher, giving me a detention, and I've felt like a naughty student all day.

Just because she reckons I'm here because of my family name.

That I'm not a real teacher.

"I can do this," I repeat to myself as I lock the car behind me and step up to the front doors of the hotel. It's night, and it's a bit chilly outside. Despite that, I've decided to wear a nice dress, although I'm worried that the cleavage is a bit low. I can feel the cold wind whip freely across my exposed breasts. I do look *good*, though. It's the one thing getting me through tonight, the one thing getting me through Miss Tweed's disgusting lecture from this morning.

I look damn good in this dress.

As I reach the front steps of the hotel, someone comes out of nowhere and jumps in front of me. I'm surprised by the sudden movement and it takes me a moment to recognize who it is.

Mr. Brown. The school principal of Poseidon's Academy.

Jesus.

What a shock.

At five-foot-eight, I'm pretty tall for a woman, and Mr. Brown, at five-foot-seven, is pretty short for a man, so it's a weird imbalance for me to have to look down at my boss, at a man much older than me.

"Miss Finn," Mr. Brown says as he jumps in front of me. He's blocking my way into the hotel.

"Mr. Brown! I didn't expect to see you outside. Shouldn't you be in the hotel talking to the guests?"

He straightens up, but he's still shorter than me. "I wanted to talk to you privately before you went in," he replies.

Oh, no. This doesn't sound good.

"Sure, go ahead."

My Brown is a nervous man. I can tell he doesn't like the social aspects of his job. He's more than happy to sit behind his desk and fiddle with numbers all day and not talk directly to his staff. He always puts me on edge when I talk to him with all his little twitches and nervous ticks. I do like him though. He's a decent man, although very much under the power of Miss Tweed and her dominating personality. It's almost like she runs the school and Mr.

Brown is her personal assistant. He never fights back at her. To him, Miss Tweed's word is Gospel.

A lot of staff have left in the years between me leaving Poseidon's Academy as a student and me returning as a teacher. Mr. Brown became the principal just a few months after I graduated, so it's good we don't have that weird student-teacher dynamic I still have with one or two other staff who used to teach me.

"How can I put this delicately? I'll be blunt, if I may," Mr. Brown starts, beckoning me to the side of the hotel, away from any incoming guests. He speaks to me in an anxious, hushed voice. "The school is, as you may know, in a bit of a difficult situation at the moment, money-wise. We really need some emergency cash, to put it frankly."

"I've heard."

"Ah, good. Well, that's why these fundraisers are so important. You are a, uh, very charming woman, Miss Finn. I hope we can rely on you to talk to everyone here tonight."

I nod my head. I just want to get out of this awkward conversation. I need to find the nearest glass of Chardonnay ASAP. "Of course."

"Good. Good. So, please, talk to everyone. It's so very, very important."

"Okay, Mr. Brown. Understood."

"Great, go get that money," he chuckles. "Have a good night. I'll see you in there."

"Sure."

He takes out a packet of cigarettes from his jacket pocket. "Filthy habit, I know. But it calms the nerves."

I smile at him and quickly dash inside the hotel, wanting to get away from the very high cringe levels of awkwardness. I know Mr. Brown would absolutely *love* it if I got my dad involved in the fundraising for the school; that's probably why I'm always roped in on these fundraiser nights. He and Miss Tweed would be over the moon if I used my family money to make a private donation to Poseidon's Academy but, like I told them on my first day, I won't ever want to use my family's wealth in my career. I've separated myself totally from my father's wealth. Not that I'm ashamed of it or anything, it's just that I want to make my own way in the world and not rely on family for everything. I've been already lucky enough to receive a top-tier education at Poseidon's Academy when I was a student. I don't need - or want - to use my family's wealth as a crutch for the rest of my life.

I follow the signs and head inside the hotel conference room, frantically adjusting my dress to make sure my nipples don't pop out. The room's pretty full by the time I enter. It seems like every other member of staff is already there.

I spot that Miss Tweed's surrounded by a swarm of parents. They always love talking to her. She's all smiles when it comes to parents. She can put on such a fake act when she wants to, when she smells money.

I make a beeline straight for the wine. Chardonnay. My favorite. I snatch a glass from the table and take a sip. Refreshing. Some Dutch courage is definitely needed for the night ahead.

I start talking to a local businessman. Some old guy in a suit. We've chatted before. He says he's very keen to donate some money to the school, so he's been to most of the school's fundraisers thus far. To be honest, I think he's more in it to ogle at my tits, which he does during our entire conversation. I don't think he even looks me in the eyes once. It's like he's talking to my cleavage as if my boobs are a separate person to the rest of my body.

This is turning out to be a very fun night indeed.

I receive a tap on my shoulder as I talk to the businessman, snapping him out of rambling about *PC culture gone mad* at my tits.

"Miss Finn!" The person who's tapped me is very enthusiastic. I can tell by the sound of their voice it's Mr. Brown. "Miss Finn!" He taps again and I turn around, happy to get my breasts away from the local businessman's intense focus.

"Yes, Mr. Brown?"

"You have just got to meet the most charming man." Mr. Brown gestures behind him to a man standing with his back turned to us. "Miss Finn, I want to introduce you to Mr. Deep."

The man turns.

And my heart drops.

Mr. Deep?

That must mean-

Skipper Deep.

Skipper Deep is standing in front of me.

Mr. Brown is introducing me to Skipper Deep.

No.

Skipper's holding a glass of red wine in one hand. His brown eyes scan me and my dress up and down. He then smiles at me. His stupid gorgeous smile.

And my heart drops even further.

For the second time this month, Skipper Deep is standing in front of me in an expensive tailored suit and is *smiling* at me.

What the hell is going on?

For the second time this month, I'm trapped into speaking to Skipper *fucking* Deep. In the same *fucking* hotel conference room my brother and sister-in-law got married in.

He really is like a ghost from my past, haunting me.

Skipper winks at me and nods at Mr. Brown. "Oh, don't

worry, sir. Miss Finn and I went to Poseidon's Academy together. We were actually in the same class. We're old friends, isn't that right, Miss Finn?"

I gulp.

I don't respond.

Mr. Brown's face lights up. I can see he's overjoyed by this news. He doesn't observe how uncomfortable I am; his vision is blinded by Skipper's wealth. "That's great! Well, maybe Miss Finn can run you over what we're currently doing at the school, and her role in it," he turns to me. "Mr. Deep is here as a potential *investor* into the school, looking to buy a share in it."

"An investor?"

What?

He's a potential investor? He doesn't just want to donate, but he actually wants to buy part of the school?

What the hell's going on?

Skipper casually takes a sip of his wine. It shades his lips darker red. *Kissable* red. "Yes, I'm looking at investing in my old school. I had some great memories there, Mr. Brown." He's staring at me as he says this, and I know what memories he's talking about. Memories that make my pussy wet just thinking about. Memories that come into my late-night fantasies. Memories only Skipper and I could share. "I'm sure Miss Finn can fill me in on the details of the school as it is now. We have lots to talk about."

"Oh, I'm sure you do have lots to talk about. Lots and lots, so I'll leave you two at it." Mr. Brown turns and quickly leaves with a wink towards me. It's the first time I actually don't want to see the back of the man.

I turn to Skipper. He's still smiling at me.

I'm well and truly trapped here.

God damn, I hate this man. But he does look so handsome in a suit. And he's so tall. Dark and tall and handsome, my right kind of weakness.

And his smug face betrays that he knows it.

"What are you doing here? Wasn't last week enough for you?" I ask Skipper quietly so that Mr. Brown or Miss Tweed don't overhear.

He smirks at me. "My room's upstairs. I'm staying at the hotel. That's why I'm here."

I roll my eyes. He knows mentioning his room might get me a little bit hot under the collar.

And, by God, it's working.

No, don't think about him that way.

Remember what he did to you, remember the pain he put you under.

"Don't you dare start talking to me about your bedroom. What are you *really* doing here, Skipper?"

"Like I told your principal, I'm here to think about investing in my old school."

"Why?" I ask, spluttering. "Invest?"

Skipper shakes his head at me like I'm just a stupid schoolgirl who needs to be taught something simple. "I'm shocked you haven't Facebook stalked me, Miss Finn."

"Why would I?"

"Curiosity? Maybe you'll want to know what I've been up to all these years?"

"I really don't care, Skipper."

"Well, if you did, you'd find out my family's main business in America is in education, particularly in private schools. We're looking to expand our education investment portfolio into Australia and Poseidon's Academy is, naturally, the first place I thought of as a trial run."

"You're thinking of buying up a part of the school *I* work in?"

Skipper takes another sip of his red wine and winks at me. "Exactly."

"You're a bastard."

"Maybe I am, but I remember you *really* liking that when we were eighteen," he says. He gestures at my low-cut dress. "By the way, you're looking very nice tonight. Stylish and sexy, that sums you up."

I roll my eyes again. God, he is very charming when he wants to be. "Thanks."

He very nearly makes me think of him as a normal, decent person.

"My room is only upstairs if you want to jump back into things."

And there he goes again, right back to being a bastard.

"Skipper, what you did to me was so wrong. I told you last week I never want to see you again. Why can't you get that through your thick skull?"

"Well, that's going to be difficult."

"How so?"

"Your principal has invited me to stay in New Water and inspect the school before I make a decision whether or not to invest."

"What?"

"See what's going on."

"You're going to stay here?"

"Oh, yes."

"You can't."

"I am."

"You're going to be in the school, checking out the classes?"

Skipper continues like he hasn't just dropped a bombshell. "I really do hope the past can be the past between us, Miss Finn. I wouldn't want it to come between our professional... relationship."

Relationship? Professional? What is he talking about?

He's here to inspect the school? Inspect my workplace?

"Let's get one thing straight here, Skipper. I'm never *ever* going to allow you to inspect my classroom." My voice shakes as I come to terms with what he's saying here.

He's here for one thing, to screw me over for a second time. I know it.

I'm not going to give him the satisfaction of seeing me so shocked.

I turn around and storm away from him, heading back to the white wine table. I grab a new glass and head over to chat to a group of parents I already know, all the time wary of the man. Skipper doesn't follow me. *Good.*

I need to get away from him, just like I did at the wedding.

He wants to invest in the school?

He wants to inspect the school?

Inspect me? Judge the job I'm doing?

No. Freaking. Way.

I'm not going to let him.

Not a chance in hell.

Skipper Deep may have a hold over my deep, dark fantasies, but right now, above everything else, I want him out of my school, out of my town, and out of my life.

7

EIGHT YEARS AGO

SANDY

Inside the car, I apply the lipstick to my lips. Bright red. All done with the makeup, I check myself out in the rearview mirror.

I look *good*.

"Okay, I can do this," I say to myself in the reflection. "You look sexy as hell, Sandy."

Pep talk over, I adjust my top so that my cleavage is showing at its best angle and I step out of my car. It's dark out; the only lights on in the street are coming from the house I've parked in front of. Thudding club music echoes from inside. I'm here for a house party and I think I've found the right house. It's gotta be this one.

I'm here for a surprise.

My boyfriend, Skipper Deep, thinks I'm at home studying for the end of high-school exams. My Shakespeare

English exam. I *love* Shakespeare, especially his romances. Romeo and Juliet is right on top of that list. I want to become a teacher, preferably for English. Nothing will satisfy me more than passing on my love of Shakespeare and words to the next generation. I'm a bit of a geek, so usually, I would be sitting at home studying on a Saturday night, but tonight's an exception. Tonight's the night I'll surprise my boyfriend at this house party. He thinks he's here on his own, that I'm not coming as usual, that I'm studying at home, being the geek that I am.

But no.

This time, I'm going to actually come to the party. Surprise him.

I'm going to blow his mind.

He's the party boy and I'm the nerdy girl - well, with this lipstick I'm the *sexy* nerdy girl, the same nerdy girl who's gonna let her hair down and have a good night.

My phone buzzes in my handbag as I leave the car. It's my best friend, Nicole.

Hey hun! You sure you're not coming out tonight? Xx

I chuckle softly to myself. She and my boyfriend have been pushing me at school all week to come out tonight and I have rejected them at every turn. They really, really think I'm not coming out to this party tonight.

Suckers.

Sorry I can't! Busy studying. You know me! Xx

She replies straight away.

Awww you're such a little goody-two-shoes geek. Have fun with your textbooks. I'm gonna have fun with some bottles of vodka xx

I laugh and throw my phone back into my handbag.

Yep, Nicole and Skipper have absolutely no idea that I'm coming tonight.

It's a big deal that I am actually going to a house party.

I can't wait to see the surprise on their faces when they see me.

We're all in the last year of high school, so why not go to a house party at least once? Why not make your last year memorable when you've spent all this time studying? It's time to let this geeky girl's hair down.

I also want to do something cute for Skipper. Something sexy. Tonight, I want to have some proper dirty sex with him. Down and rough. I know he'll love that. I mean, I've even washed and shaved myself and everything. I'm all ready for some hot fun.

Can't wait.

I skip into the house, ready to surprise. The place inside is busy and even louder than I expected. Neon lighting everywhere. It seemed like the whole school was there, drinking and partying.

Huh, so this is what I've been missing out on whilst studying Elizabethan playwrights?

I search through the living room, recognizing faces from school and family friends. This place is bigger and even busier than I'd initially thought it'd be. I wander around, twisting my neck looking for the gorgeous face of my boyfriend. I try looking for his smile, his smile that can melt me in a heartbeat. I can't find him anywhere. There are so many people about. I walk into the center of the room, aka the makeshift dance floor, to get a better view. Still no sign of Skipper anywhere. Maybe he's left already?

"Hey, you." The voice is familiar. Someone pats me on the back. It's Cliff, my cousin. "Fancy seeing you here!"

"I thought I'd make the effort for once," I say to him, blushing at my dress.

"You look beautiful, Sandy," my cousin says. He has a trail of friends behind him. He's clearly the alpha of the group. He's athletic and tall, just like my younger brother

Cove. Don't want to brag, but good genes run in our family. "Do you want a beer?"

He offers me a plastic cup full of dark liquid and I shake my head. Beer's not really my thing, I prefer white wine. "No, thanks."

"I guess you're looking for Skipper?"

My eyes widen. "Yes, have you seen him?"

Cliff nods. "Yeah, but ages ago and only in passing. He went upstairs, I think. I didn't get much of a chance to speak to him."

"Thanks," I say, scurrying off. Cliff starts yelling at one of his friends behind me. I think he's calling for some shots. I laugh to myself. Cliff's always been the leader. He's always up to do a round of shots.

He's one bad boy, Cliff. A real heartbreaker. A playboy. All he wants to do is get out of town and see the world - well, more like he wants to get out of town and see some international pussy.

It'll take a girl with balls of steel to nail down that bastard.

I head up the massive staircase to the next floor. This is where the bedrooms and bathrooms are. There are fewer partygoers up here. Maybe Skipper is having a deep conversation with a friend? Maybe that's why he's up here?

I pass the queue to the toilet and into the hallway leading into the bedrooms.

"Skipper?" I call out down the hallway, hoping to hear an answer. Nothing.

I head down the hallway and listen at each door.

Fuck it.

Cliff did say he saw Skipper head up here.

I open up the first bedroom. A group of stoners are gathered around a bong, all sitting on the big king-sized bed. As

I enter, they all turn and look at me, their eyes red from smoking a bit too much on the good stuff.

"Oops, sorry," I mutter and hastily close the door on them.

I continue down the hallway to the next bedroom. I know what I'm doing is a bit bad, but it is a party and I know that Skipper is here somewhere. Maybe he's smoking some weed? I wouldn't mind if he was. I just want to see him. I want him to see how sexy I look in this dress.

I open this door to the next bedroom.

"Skipper?"

It takes me a moment to understand what's going on, and when I do, my whole world comes crashing down.

No.

Skipper, my boyfriend, is in the bed with Nicole, my best friend.

They're both naked.

They both turn to me, irritated that a partygoer has broken into their room. But then they both recognize it's me and they freeze.

"Sandy?" Skipper asks, his face reddening. "What are you doing here? I thought you're at home?"

I just stare at them both in disbelief.

The color drains from my face.

My fist hardens around the door handle.

I can't believe what I'm seeing.

"Sandy," Nicole whispers. "I'm so sorry."

I came all this way for you to see me looking sexy, Skipper.

"We're drunk, Sandy," Skipper offers as way of explanation. It's pathetic.

"It doesn't matter," I reply quietly. "This is wrong."

Skipper bows his head. "We've been drinking. We

never meant for this to happen. One thing led to another, that's all."

That's all?

Unbelievable.

No matter what he says, he can't get out of this. Not this one.

I take in a deep breath. Everything is crashing down around me, but I still have enough clarity of thought to spew forth my next statement.

"I never want to see you, Skipper, or you, Nicole, ever again. Ever, *ever* again. You got me?"

They blink back at me, but they've got the message.

I don't say anything else. I *can't* say anything else. I turn straight out and sprint down the stairs and back into my car.

I don't stop.

I don't breathe.

I don't cry, I just drive on home.

My whole world has collapsed.

And that was the last time I saw Skipper Deep. I never spoke to Nicole again. And she kept her distance from me until we finished high school. I've never seen her since. She knew better than to try to talk to me about it.

And Skipper, that was the last time I ever saw him.

The last time I saw him until the day of my brother's wedding when he decided to walk across the room to talk to me.

The last time before tonight at the school fundraiser, when he got my boss to introduce him to me.

And now he's back in town, and he wants to work with me.

He moved to England straight after that house party, out of my life until he came back eight years later. He went off and became a success in his family's company, investing and owning elite private schools in America, and now he wants to invest in the very place I work.

He's back in my life, and I don't know how to feel about it.

But one thing's for sure, that memory of that house party eight years ago still remains firmly in my mind.

It's going to take a lot for me to talk to, *to even trust*, Skipper Deep again.

8

SKIPPER

No GIRL HAS EVER COMPARED to Sandy Finn. No girl. Trust me, I've spent the last few years screwing around, dating all the time, picking up so many women from expensive bars and parties all over the world, and yet no girl has even come close to what it was like with Sandy. I've tried them all. I've tried to screw enough girls to get Sandy out of my head, but so far, I've been completely and utterly unsuccessful.

I fucked up eight years ago. That sudden drunk impulse to fuck Nicole at that stupid house party has scarred me for life. That night - the night of my dumb decision - I lost Sandy. Seemingly forever. I lost the one person who meant the world to me.

And I've regretted it ever since.

I want her back.

I *need* her back.

I'm going to get her back.

I watch her storm away from me at the fundraiser. She in that pretty dress of hers. That very low-cut dress. Sandy, despite being a book-loving geek, always knew how to look her very best on a night out. Seeing her tonight looking like that made me horny in ways I haven't been for years.

The only girl in the world for me.

I take a sip of my red wine to look casual, to not look like Sandy has ripped my heart out as she turned away from me.

Bide your time, there's going to be plenty more chances to talk to her.

During our whole conversation together, it was nearly impossible not to imagine ripping off that dress, putting my mouth between her slender legs, and tasting her pussy. I had to actively make sure my eyes were focused on her eyes and not on her perfectly round tits as she insulted me at the fundraiser.

And now she's run off for the second time.

It's okay. It's what I expected.

I knew she'll be pissed off initially when she heard I was to spend some time investigating the school. I understand what she must be feeling, but I still see that spark in her when she sees me. I know, deep down, she wants me. We just have to resolve what happened eight years ago, that's all.

I have to make her see that I'm no longer that boy who fucked her over.

Sure, I am looking to expand my family's education business empire into Australia, but really the whole thing is a bit of a ruse. I could've gone to any number of elite schools in the country, but I chose Poseidon's Academy for a reason. And it isn't for nostalgia.

Sandy works there.

And I'm here to get her.

That's all.

That's why I'm really here.

For Sandy.

I really did fuck up eight years ago, and now I'm here to apologize, but I don't know how. I know Sandy would never, not in a million years, accept some half-hearted apology from me. She's too strong for that. No, this apology has to mean something.

It has to come from my heart.

I watch her from across the room as I get a refill of my wine. She's so natural, so radiant. It's like she glows at me wherever she is. My eyes are always attracted to her. She's all I want. Her laugh is infectious. Her body is to die for. Man, I want her.

But Sandy is smart, another reason why I fell for her. If I want her back, I know I have to put in the hard work. She's so smart and fiercely independent. She's not just gonna fall for me just because I rock up back into her life and mumble a pitiful *sorry*. I'm gonna have to do better than that to get her back. Much better.

She's worth everything.

Seeing her again tonight has filled me with renewed hope. I know, behind her tough exterior, she really does have those same feelings for me as she did eight years ago. I've just got to coax it out of her. I'm gonna really have to work hard.

Damn, I just *miss* her so much. It's hard to even just look at her.

I take a long drink of my wine and try not to think about how much my heart longs for that woman across the room.

"Hello, you must be Mr. Deep." Someone appears at my side. It's a short older woman. The first thing I notice is her massive puffy hair. It probably takes up a third of her height. She's wearing a lot of makeup. Her perfume is strong. Very strong. It tickles my nose and makes me want to cough.

"Yes, I am. Skipper Depp, nice to meet you. And you are?" I offer my hand and she shakes it.

The older woman smiles at me and tilts her head inquisitively. "I am Miss Tweed, the head of mathematics at Poseidon's Academy."

"Nice to meet you."

"Mr. Brown's told me *everything* about you," she says.

"Really?"

"That you're looking to invest in the school."

"I am."

"Well, you're speaking to the right person, Mr. Deep," Miss Tweed explains, her eyes lighting up. She takes a step closer to me, still smiling, and places her hand on my arm. "I am the bookkeeper of the school. The head of the money. I'm basically the brains behind the institution."

"Are you?"

"Yes. I know everything about what there is to know about Poseidon's Academy. All the gossip, all the financial records, all the important things."

I nod in agreement. "They're good things to know if I'm going to invest."

She giggles at my comment. "Exactly. That's why you need me." I'm not an idiot and I can see when someone's really trying to butter me up. With my family's business and wealth, it's something I've dealt with a lot over the years. Miss Tweed's a pro at it, though. I gotta give her that. She really has the vocal tone, and the smile perfected to a T.

"So, you're the person I should come to?"

"One hundred percent, Mr. Deep. You can come to me *any* time you want, for anything. I'll always be available to you. Whenever you want, you can talk to me." She rubs my arm and flutters her eyelashes at me.

"That's really good to know," I reply.

"In any way I can, I'll help you, Mr. Deep."

"I really like your necklace." I gesture towards her big pearl necklace. Miss Tweed glances down at it, blushing.

"Oh, this silly old thing?"

"It's very nice."

"Thank you, Mr. Deep."

I'm thinking of making an excuse and walking away, but an idea pops into my head.

"May I ask you a question now about the school?" I ask Miss Tweed.

She loves this. "Absolutely. Go ahead."

"That teacher over there," I point at Sandy amongst the group of parents she's talking to. Miss Tweed nods.

"That's Sandy Finn, the English teacher."

"What do you think of her?"

Miss Tweed turns back to me, the smile gone from her face. "Do you want the truth, Mr. Deep?"

"Sure."

"The young Miss Finn should've been... let go from the school a long time ago, if I must say so myself. I've tried pressurizing Mr. Brown, but it's been a long process."

Wow.

"Fire her? What for?"

It's obvious Miss Tweed knows nothing about my and Sandy's personal connection.

"She's not a *real* teacher, Mr. Deep. She's here on nepotism grounds. You see, I don't know if you know but Miss Finn's family are very rich. She insists that her father has nothing to do with her financially, but I'm sure that's still the case. No one's that selfless."

"And what's so wrong about her?"

"Trust me, Mr. Deep, I've seen her in action in the classroom. She can't teach, it's that simple. She can't maintain discipline and order. It's because of her that I worry that her students are going to fail English come the exams this year. I mean, even today I had to break out a fight between her students that had erupted into the school hallways and were disrupting other classes. She should be fired."

"I see."

"If I were put in charge of Poseidon's Academy, I would be making some big changes immediately," Miss Tweed continues. "Changes for the better. I'd be cutting the riff-raff, so to speak. The first to go would be Miss Finn over there."

"Interesting," I reply. "Well, I'm sure I'll be talking to you a lot over the next few weeks."

"Oh, it'll be so good having you around, Mr. Deep."

I watch Miss Tweed waddle away. She slowly makes her way around the hotel conference room until she's talking to the same group of parents Sandy is with. It's like she wants to intimidate Sandy with her presence. God, that teacher has really got it out for Sandy.

I'll need to keep an eye on her.

So, she can't wait to start cutting the riff-raff. Very interesting. It'll be good to find out more about this Miss Tweed.

But my attention quickly darts away from her and onto Sandy. She's laughing with a parent. God, she's beautiful. I steady myself with another sip of wine. She has only got more mesmerizing eight years later. I've made a good choice coming back here for her. She's just like she is in my dreams.

The only girl in the world for me.

My focus is distracted by someone coming towards me. A young woman about my age is sauntering towards me.

She's very conventionally attractive. Black hair. Big lips. Very skimpy dress.

She walks right up to me and offers her hand. "Hey," she says. "I'm Becky. Becky Taylor."

What now?

9

SANDY

I SAW HER APPROACH HIM.

Becky Taylor.

The most attractive female parent of the school, who also happens to be a young single parent. *Single* being the operative word there.

I saw Becky Taylor sauntering across the room, shaking her hips with every step like a supermodel on a runway, all the way towards Skipper until she was introducing herself to him. Fluttering her eyelashes. Perking up her big tits. I saw Skipper shake her hand and start to chat with her.

Bloody hell.

He didn't have a chance to get away, even if he wanted to.

Of course, she would be all over him. Becky had a special gift of being able to sniff out rich eligible bachelors. It was her superpower. A lot of the single male parents had been on the receiving end of her powers plenty of times, and none emerged from her captivity unscathed. I bet even

Skipper Deep will find it hard to untangle himself from her claws.

And now she was deploying her full sensual arsenal against Skipper. I shake my head.

Wait, why am I jealous?

Was that really a pang of jealously that passed through me when I saw her talking to him?

Why should I care?

Was I actually envious of Becky Taylor talking to Skipper so seductively? Flirting with him? Why should I even care who he talks to? He's not my boyfriend.

But I do feel envious. I do feel a touch of panic as Becky Taylor flirts with Skipper. I want to go over there and push her out of the way. He's mine.

No.

NO.

I can't be jealous of her. Skipper Deep is not my boyfriend. He screwed me over all those years ago, and now I want nothing to do with him. Seeing him in bed, with my *best friend*, all those years ago, completely devastated me to the point that he nearly ruined everything. I want nothing to do with him ever again. I'm *supposed* to be angry he's waltzed back into my life like he has with no care for my feelings, I shouldn't be jealous of some attractive single mother with big tits talking to him.

I should not be caring about this nearly as half as I currently am.

But I still can't take my eyes off my former lover. I still can't get him, or his naked body, out of my head. His hung cock. My memories.

No. Stop it, Sandy.

Have I really reverted back to being a giddy schoolgirl with a crush?

A crush on *Skipper Deep?* The man who betrayed my

trust, the man who ruined the last year of high school for me?

God, Sandy. You're so stupid.

"So, Miss Finn, how are you feeling about the exams?"

My attention shoots back to the group of the parents I've been talking to when I escaped from Skipper earlier. They surround me in a semi-circle, waiting for my response. Miss Tweed has joined the conversation and now she's asking me a question. I forgot what it was; I was too focused on that Becky talking to Skipper.

"Pardon?" I ask.

"The exams," Miss Tweed repeats, her usual patronizing smile plastered over her face. "How are you feeling about them? They're very important for the students, and for *you*."

Ugh. Don't talk to me like I'm stupid.

"Yeah, I'm feeling pretty good about the exams," I reply. I turn to include all the listening parents. "We actually started on Romeo and Juliet today. It's my favorite of all Shakespeare's plays. Two households and all that. It's so romantic and, yet, tragic."

There's a murmur of approval from the gathered parents. They love it when I talk about classic literature. Miss Tweed doesn't look pleased with how I handled that question. I've outshone her.

Good. Suck it up.

"Well, I have a feeling mathematics will be the top average class this year in the exams," Miss Tweed remarks loudly, scanning her beady brown eyes over the parents. She wants them to pay attention to her. "I've worked them extra hard this year. I pride myself on my students' marks and how well they do every year. Mathematics is the cornerstone of a good education. We can all sit around reading stories all day to our heart's content, but mathematics is what expands a young child's mind."

Another round of approval from the parents and I take a drink from my wine. Miss Tweed absolutely loves the sound of her own voice.

"And if you will please excuse me," the teacher says, nodding towards me. "I need to have a private word with Miss Finn here. Lovely to meet you all. Hopefully, you can all speak to Mr. Brown and donate tonight."

She takes me by the arm and pulls me away from the group. She's all smiles at the parents, but I feel her cold, hard grip around my arm digging into me. Her fingers are like talons. She drags me away to a corner of the hotel conference room so that we're safely out of earshot from everyone else.

"What's wrong?" I ask, pulling my arm away from Miss Tweed's grip.

"You see that man over there?" She points a bony finger towards Skipper. He's still talking to Becky. She's placed her slender hand on his shoulder and is *incredibly* close to his tall body. He doesn't look uncomfortable at all, despite how they're nearly touching. Well, he's always been a massive flirt, so they're perfect together. But, despite my anger, another pang of jealousy runs through my heart.

Please stop talking to her.

"Yeah, that's Skipper Finn," I say to the teacher.

"Good that you know who he is," Miss Tweed continues. "And I'm sure that you know why he's here, don't you? It is absolutely imperative that he invests in our school. We need those finances under control."

"Yeah."

Miss Tweed pats me on the shoulder. "So, don't neglect him. He's the most important donor we've ever come across. The richest I've seen. The school's best potential investor."

"Right."

"And he is a very lovely man. I've just had the loveliest conversation with him. Oh, he's very handsome. He even commented on my pearl necklace. How sweet of him. I think he really likes me."

I take another sip of my wine. I've been in too many uncomfortable and downright awkward conversations tonight for my liking. I just want to go home. "Okay."

"So, how about you work the room a bit harder, hm? An attractive little airhead like you shouldn't let her only talents go to waste. Remember, the school is on the line here."

Attractive little airhead?

What the fuck?

Miss Tweed pats me one more time on the shoulder and strolls back over to the round of parents.

I can't say anything to her. She's more senior than me at the school. I can't yell or shout or lecture her about referring to me as nothing but an attractive airhead. No one else overheard, no other witnesses. I'd be treated as hysterical. It's her word against mine.

And she intimidates the *hell* out of me.

Miss Tweed's out to get me; I know that now. She doesn't just want me gone; she wants to *humiliate* me. Destroy me completely. I am at a loss for words after her casual insult. She's a monster.

I take a nervous sip of my wine.

And Skipper is still talking to Becky.

Can this day get even worse?

Wow. She's really trying her best with him.

I watch him as he evades her advances. He's so confident, so smooth. He's just so damn *sure* of himself. It's so infuriating to observe, but it secretly turns me on.

Goddamn it.

Skipper Deep still turns me on even eight years after I

caught him cheating with my best friend at that house party. That night when I saw them in bed together *destroyed* my life. I hadn't properly dated or fallen for a guy since then. I know now that Skipper Deep has had a hold over my heart these past eight years, I thought I'd got rid of his control, but seeing him again at the wedding and then tonight has caused all my old feelings for him to rush back. The man was just too goddamn *charming*. The way he looked at me when we were speaking earlier. That sparkle in his deep brown eyes. He wanted me, and he didn't even care that I knew how much.

No way am I going to let my natural feelings for the man overpower me. No way am I going to let the fact that he's going to be "investigating" my place of work draw me back to him. No way am I going to fall in love with Skipper Deep again, despite what my heart wants.

If only he didn't look so deliciously handsome.

If only he never came back to New Water.

10

SANDY

"GOOD MORNING MISS FINN."

The whole class speaks in unison, in that sing-song that all kids love to do. I stand in front of the students in my classroom and gesture for them to sit down at their desks. I smile and lean forward.

"Okay, we started at a rocky start last lesson, so how about we begin again today," I say, eyeballing both James and Tom especially. I've separated the two naughty boys to opposite sides of the classroom where, hopefully, there won't be a chance for any more fights to break out. If anything happens that's in any way like the crazy fight the other day when they spilled out into the school hallway and punches were thrown, then I know I'll have to kiss my career as a teacher goodbye. The paperwork I had to fill out in the aftermath was bigger than the Bible, and twice as hard to read, so let's hope the two boys can sit quietly on opposite sides of the room peacefully. Let's hope that there's no more bleeding noses. "We have a big exam coming up, so

I want you all to listen. We need to do well in these exams, right?"

No reaction from the class.

Great.

We're back to square one, I see.

"So, Shakespeare. You may all think he's a scary writer and that you don't understand his plays, but once you do, your eyes will be open to a whole new world. Trust me. How about we start at the beginning of Romeo and Juliet?"

One of the students, a girl named Annie in the front row, puts her hand up.

FINALLY! Some enthusiasm.

"Yes, Annie?" I ask, happy that one of my students is actively taking an interest in English.

"There's a man at the door," Annie says.

Right.

We all turn our heads to the classroom door, and I see that Annie's right. A man is indeed peering into the door's window.

I gulp.

I know who that man is.

Skipper Deep.

Fucking hell.

Skipper opens the door and steps inside.

Inside *my* classroom.

He's wearing another suit from the one at the fundraiser the other night. This one seems equally expensive. Nice and tailored. The man definitely knows how to wear clothes. He's freshly shaved. His perfect jawline shouldn't be real.

Why does he have to saunter in like this, into my class-room, looking as handsome as he does? Why can't he just disappear from my life and not add any more problems to my full plate?

Why doesn't he just buzz off?

"Sorry for interrupting, Miss Finn," he says, raising his hands up in mock surrender. My students just gawk at him, speechless. "Don't mind me everyone, I'm just watching."

Just watching?

I don't think so.

"Excuse me, Skipper," I start to say, but he immediately cuts me off.

"Sorry, it's Mr. Deep at school."

Why...

I bristle at him in rage. I think my students can see my face go suddenly red in anger. "Okay, *Mr. Deep.* This is a private class. What are you doing in here?"

Skipper pulls out a pen and notepad from his jacket and flashes them exaggeratedly to the class and me. "I'm just taking some notes."

"Taking notes?"

"Really, don't mind me, I'm just here to observe like we spoke about the other night." He nods at me like everything is normal. Like *this* intrusion is normal.

It really isn't.

He's not welcome here.

The other night? Obviously, he's talking about the fundraiser. He's talking about how he's here to inspect the school.

I thought I told him never to inspect my classroom.

I thought I made that pretty clear.

I know why he's here. I mean, *come on*, there's no way he actually *wants* to listen in to my class. He's here in my classroom for one reason, and one reason only; to annoy me. Piss me off. I hate him and his stupidly gorgeous face. I hate how he's decided to single me out.

I stand in front of the classroom and shake my head at Skipper as he makes his way to an empty chair at the back of the room. He leisurely sits down and clicks his pen, then he looks up at me with an expectant face, waiting for me to start. The entire room is silent as all the kids watch him. They glance back at me, waiting for my reaction.

Is this a joke?

My God, the man is *exhausting*.

This must be a lot of fun for my students. It's obvious something's up between Skipper and me.

"Please," he says to me across the classroom, across my class. "Please continue. Sorry for my interruption. Just pretend I'm not here."

Oh, if he wants me to pretend he's not here, then I'm going to play his game. The man just can't come into my classroom and expect me to bow down at his feet. Not in my classroom.

There's no way to get rid of him without causing a scene in front of my students, so I'm just going to completely ignore him. Really pretend he's not here.

I can be irritating too, Mr. Deep.

"So," I start up again, talking now to my students. Some have turned their attention back to me, some are still staring at Skipper in the back. "Let's start."

I describe the basic plot of Romeo and Juliet to the class. I talk to them about the story, the characters, and the setting. I try to make it imaginative and creative, acting out certain scenes. I want my students engaged in Shakespeare, just like I'd been at their age. I want them all to pass the big exams that are coming up. Seeing myself do well at academic tests at school was so encouraging to me when I was a student. It was life-changing. Passing those exams taught me that, if I set my mind to something and work hard enough, I can achieve anything. I want my own students to experience the same feeling, to come away from my class knowing that they too can achieve anything they wanted.

I come to the end of my overview of the play, noticing that Skipper has been writing in his notepad the entire time. I try to ignore him, but it's very difficult when you have a six-foot-one beautiful man sitting in your back row making notes about you.

I wonder what he's writing.

"So, any questions?" I ask. No one's put up their hands except for someone in the back. Skipper. Of course. His hand's raised, but I ignore him. "Anyone? Does anyone have a question about Romeo and Juliet?"

No hands raised except for Skipper's.

Please, someone. Anyone.

Just not Skipper. Anyone but Skipper.

"I have a question," he calls out from the back of the room.

I ignore him still. "Who can sum up what I said?"

"I have a question."

"Anyone want to tell me what they think of the play?"

"I have a question."

"Does anyone like the play?"

No hands up except for *his*. Some kids have turned around to look at Skipper. This is really starting to turn into a scene now. He's still got his hand up and he keeps on talking over me.

"I have a question."

I sigh.

"Okay, *Mr. Deep*. What's the question that you're so urgent to ask?"

His face is so smug it's perfectly ripe for punching.

"So," he says, leaning back in his chair with a satisfied grin. He's getting comfortable. He loves making me acknowledge him in my classroom. "Romeo and Juliet is about two teenagers who are in love, yes?"

"Yes."

"Two star-crossed lovers?"

"Yes, what's your question, Mr. Deep?"

"I'm coming to it properly. Give me a minute, Miss Finn. So, their families didn't want them together and kept them apart?"

"Yes."

Where's he going with this?

He ignores my irate tone and glare at him and continues. "And Romeo kills himself when he thinks Juliet's dead when she really isn't?"

"Yes."

"And then, finding out that he's dead, she kills herself?"

"Yes."

"So, what do you think would've happened if they didn't kill themselves?"

Really, where is he going with this?

"What do you mean?"

"Say they didn't kill themselves. What do you think would've happened?" Skipper asks. "Do you think that their families would've kept the two teenagers apart, even though they're made for each other? But then, do you think they meet, like eight years later, and rekindle their romance? But what if Juliet blames Romeo for why they had to separate, even though they're star-crossed lovers? What do you think happens then to our two heroes?"

Oh, you sly dog.

Skipper lowers his arm and shrugs at me. He winks.

He is simply *unbearable.*

He's basically just gone ahead and ripped up my favorite piece of literature to use as a crappy metaphor for our own relationship. It is kinda funny, but also so, so infuriating. He's so annoyingly cheeky to do that, it's such a Skipper thing to do. He knows all the right ways to press my buttons.

And, deep down, I like it.

Ugh, Sandy. Stop it. Remember what he did to you.

He's really on my nerves now.

Before I can say another word, the school bell rings, indicating the start of another period. The students all get up as one, collecting their things and heading out the door towards their next class as fast as their little feet can take them. I stand there in front of the whiteboard as the students stream around me to move towards the door, glaring at Skipper as he remains seated at the back of my classroom. He winks at me again and closes his notepad.

He's waiting for everyone to go.

When the last student leaves, Skipper leaps out of the chair and marches towards the door.

"That was interesting, Miss Finn."

I dive in front of him before he reaches the door, standing between him and the hallway. He's not going to leave *that* easily.

"Hang on one second, Skipper," I say, folding my arms. "We need to talk."

"Oh, do we now? I seem to recall you running away from me the other night."

"I didn't *run* away from you. I stormed out on you."

"It looked like running away to me."

"No, it wasn't running away, and today wasn't cool. You can't just rock up and listen to my classes."

"Oh, actually I can."

"You can? Says who?"

"Says Mr. Brown and Miss Tweed. Your bosses."

Of course, Miss Tweed would love him disrupting my classes.

"Really?"

"Yeah, I have to. I need to see if it's worth my time and my family's money whether or not to invest in this school."

"Really?"

"And," he says, taking a slow step towards me. He's very close. He's so tall and broad-shouldered. My mind instantly turns to thoughts about him naked, despite my better judgment. "I did want to see you in action. You were pretty good today."

I roll my eyes, faking a grunt. "I don't need you to assess my teaching abilities."

"Yeah, I know. I just want to say that you seem like a good teacher to me."

"You think?"

"I do. You've turned out great, Miss Finn. It's nice to see you doing what you always wanted to do. It's nice to see you doing what you love."

My heart flutters hearing that, but outside my expression remains stoic. He can't just come in and say some pretty words and expect me to fall into his arms. That's not how this is going to work, no matter how much he wants it to.

"Those are nice words, Skipper."

"I mean those words, Miss Finn," he takes another step towards me until we're just an inch away from touching. He reaches out and undoes my crossed arms with his soft hands. I let him. I'm breathing heavily. I'm intoxicated by how close he is. Memories flood back into my body. Memories of kissing him. Touching him. Memories of doing some very bad things in this very room. "How about I get you that drink?"

"A drink," I stutter back. I'm reminded of all those times he used to hold me in his arms. The way he used to use me during sex. The way I *loved* it. "A drink, like a date?"

He smiles his cheeky smile. "You can call it that if you want."

"So, it's not work-related?"

"No. The last time I checked, I wasn't your student, if that's what you're asking."

"I'm not."

"This isn't some weird student-teacher thing, although I'm up for playing with that in the bedroom."

"Shut up."

"So, is that a yes to the drink?"

I blush. He's so incredibly close to me. If I move forward even a tiny bit, we'd be kissing.

"Will this get you off my back? Out of my classes?" I ask.

"Sure."

"You promise."

He laughs. "Yes, I promise, only if you go out with me."

"One time?"

"Yes."

"Fine then. One drink."

Skipper's smile immediately transforms into a wide grin.

"Perfect. I know a great place," he says. "It's called Rockpool."

I roll my eyes at the name. "I know that restaurant. It's my cousin's."

"What? Your cousin Cliff?"

"The very same."

"Cliff owns Rockpool?"

"Yeah, he does."

"How is he? The last time I saw him must've been..."

"Eight years ago at that house party."

Skipper smiles at me. "Shit. Yeah, that'll be it," he says under his breath. "How is he?"

"I honestly don't know where Cliff is. The last I heard from him is that he's fucking his way through half the female population in Europe."

Skipper sighed. "That's typical Cliff. Always a play-boy," he says. "So, Rockpool, do you have a problem with it, then? Especially it being your cousin's place."

"No," I reply sternly. "As long as we're not eating. This is just a drink. One drink. It's not a date."

"Sure," he says. "Not a date. One drink."

"One drink."

"Let's meet there tonight."

11

SANDY

THERE'S a knock on my door. I go to open it and Skipper is standing there. His eyes light up when he sees me.

"Jesus, Sandy, you look *amazing*."

I blush, but I know it's true. I do look amazing. I'm wearing my favorite dress. It's blue, matching my eyes, and tight in all the right places to show off my curves. I've done my long blonde hair into soft glam curls. My makeup is on point. I was shocked myself looking in the mirror. I really do look amazing.

"You don't scrub up too bad yourself," I reply, and that is also true. Skipper is in yet another suit.

Where does he get all these suits and where does he keep them?

Just like all his others, this one is also perfectly tailored to show off his broad shoulders and muscular body. It also looks really, really expensive. I grew up around my dad, who loves expensive suits, so I know a good one when I see one. And Skipper picks the best. His hair has been cut and there is not a strand out of place. Dress him up in armor and he would be the perfect live-action Disney prince.

"Shall we go?" he asks, offering out his arm.

"Oh, so now you're acting like a gentleman?"

"What are you saying?" he asks in mock indignation. "I'm *always* a gentleman."

"Yeah, right." I roll my eyes. "Remember, this is one drink. Not a date."

Skipper smiles at me like he knows it's not true. Like he'll somehow change my mind. "Of course. Not a date. Message received and understood, Miss Finn."

Ugh. He's so cockily annoying it turns me on.

Why do I always fall for the bad guys?

Typical Sandy Finn.

He leads me to his car, a very fancy Lamborghini. *Just a rental*, he says like it's a crap car or something and not a luxury sports car. And he drives us off to Rockpool, the restaurant. The same restaurant my cousin Cliff owns. I don't think Cliff's been back here in New Water for years. He's off gallivanting around Europe. Last time he called me, he said he was partying pretty hard in London, and I believed him. He's a typical playboy, just like all the other men in my family. Breaking hearts, still, after all these years. Never changing.

It would be nice for him to come home though. I miss him.

Skipper is a fast driver, but also incredibly smooth. He doesn't cross any road markings at all on the way to the restaurant, not once. He's immaculate in his driving, it's just that he's very fast. I watch him as we speed around the bendy roads of New Water. His face is stoic as he drives. Strong. His jawline is sharp and his eyes focused. The man's a supermodel out of a catalog, and he's only gotten more defined and handsome after eight years. *Damn.*

We arrive at the restaurant in the center of town over-looking the beaches. Skipper talks to the waiter on the way inside. He's already booked us a table. We sit in the back in one of the booths. A place private, away from the other customers.

He wants us to be left alone together.

"I'm here for just a drink," I say to the waiter when he tries to hand us food menus. He nods and hands me just the drink menu and then disappears. From across the table, Skipper stares at me from under his perfectly groomed brown hair. He *really* does think he can change my mind on my one drink policy.

Oh, he's so wrong.

"So, it's one drink and then back to my place?" he asks with a smirk.

I glare back at him. "Don't be so filthy."

"Or what are you going to do, Miss Finn? Punish me? Teach me a lesson? Put me in detention?"

"I wish I could."

"Let's go then. Back to my hotel suite."

"You'd be so lucky."

"Come on," Skipper says. He slides closer to me in the booth so that we are sitting side-by-side. "What's the issue? You've been nothing but angry at me since I've come back. Am I ever going to see the real Miss Finn, or are you going to remain pissed off at me forever?"

"The *issue*?" I ask, whispering so we can't be overheard by the other customers. "The issue is what you did eight years ago and the fact you think we can just ignore it."

Skipper bows his head so that I can no longer see his face. He goes quiet and stays like that for a long time. I nearly lean over and ask what's wrong before he sits up again. I'm shocked. I notice his eyes are actually wet, like he's actually got *tears* in them. He takes my hand in his.

"I am sorry about what happened," he softly says under his breath. "I am so sorry. You must know, it's haunted me every day of my life. There isn't a day that goes by that I don't want to get into a time machine and go back to that party and tell my drunk ass not to go through with it. One moment of stupid impulse has destroyed me inside and out every day for the rest of my life, and I know that what I do or say from now on will never reverse what happened. But I just want to say sorry to you. For everything. That's why I'm here. That's why I'm truly here."

I look at him, deep into his brown eyes, and I know he's telling the truth. I know Skipper Deep like the back of my hand, and I know when he's being certified one hundred percent genuine. There're not many times when he is, but right now is one of them. His cocky façade is down and I'm seeing the real vulnerable him. The man I fell in love with all those years ago.

He's actually sorry. Skipper Deep wants to tell me he's sorry.

"You're sorry?" I ask.

"I am."

I lean back in my seat and let go of his hand. "Wow, that's a lot to take in."

"I know."

I remember that night. Ascending those stairs in that house, opening that bedroom door. The image of Skipper and my best friend in bed together. Exposed. It comes flooding back to me like it happened yesterday.

I can't forget something that easily. Not over some nice words.

It'll take a lot more for me to trust him again.

"You better understand that this doesn't change anything between us," I say. "Just because you come back to

New Water and say you're sorry doesn't mean I'll just jump back into bed with you."

"Oh, really? Damn. That's just what I was thinking will happen." Skipper grins at me. Cheeky Skipper's back.

And he makes me laugh. I have to cover my mouth to stop myself from spitting everywhere in giggles. He knows just how to make me laugh.

It's good to see the cocky Skipper again. The vulnerable side is nice, but I prefer it when he's all confident and sure of what he wants.

And, despite his jokes, I know he wants me.

Well, even with an apology, he's going to have to work hard.

The waiter returns.

"Any decision on the drinks?" he asks.

Before I can speak, Skipper does. "I'll have your most expensive Scotch, no ice. And my friend here will have a chilled glass of your finest Chardonnay."

The waiter heads to the bar and I smile at Skipper.

"You still know my favorite drink after all these years?"

"Of course, I would, Miss Finn. Why would I not?"

"Can you stop calling me Miss Finn? It's so irritating."

"No, Miss Finn. You're a teacher. I like how the students call you that."

"Yeah, but they're my students. They have to call me that."

"I like it."

"Stop it."

"No, I think I'm gonna keep calling you that, seeing as it pisses you off so much."

"Great." For the second time that night, I roll my eyes. Yeah, he can be super annoying.

"So, what were we talking about?" Skipper asks, scratching his head in mock confusion. "Oh, yeah, I think we were talking about you coming back to my hotel suite tonight."

"We *weren't* talking about that."

"Not even a kiss?"

"No."

"A single kiss?"

"No."

"A peck on the lips?"

"No."

"Not even one teeny tiny kiss?" Skipper leans in and makes an exaggerated kissing sound with his lips. I laugh and shove his face away with my palm.

"Absolutely not. Get that thought out of your head."

The waiter returns with our drinks. A glass of white wine for me, a short glass of Scotch for Skipper. We cheer and settle back into the booth.

"This is nice, isn't it?" Skipper asks.

"Yeah, it is nice. I haven't had a good night out for a long time."

"Really? I'd have thought have the town's eligible bachelors would be lining up to date you."

I blush. "No," I stammer.

But that's not true. I've had plenty of offers of dates. It's just that none of them were Skipper Deep. But I don't tell him this. I don't want to inflate his ego.

But I know that, even after all these years, my heart's been holding out for Skipper. Even after what he did to me. Even after feeling betrayed. I just could never get the image of him out from my heart.

No man has ever compared to him.

All the kisses, all the drunk fumbles in the dark with strange men have all felt like nothing compared to Skipper. I've enjoyed the sex over the years, but nothing has made my heart flutter or my mind hazy the same way as when

Skipper used to touch me in the school classrooms when we were teenagers. No other man has ever come close to making me feel like Skipper Deep has.

And now he's back, sitting right here next to me.

"Okay, I've got an idea," I say, drinking the rest of my wine. "How about a competition?"

Skipper perks up. He's interested. "A competition? I already like the sound of that."

"Yes, but not just any competition. A drinking competition."

"Okay, damn. A drinking competition? I'm in for that. What's it gonna be?"

I lean in close to Skipper so that I can practically *taste* his delicious aftershave. I'm teasing him with my puckered lips so close to his. I can sense him going hard between his legs. "You're so desperate to make me come back to your hotel suite. How about we make that part of the deal? Let's see who can endure the most shots. If you win, I will willingly go back to yours right now and fuck you out of this world."

Skipper nods. "I like the sound of that," he says. "What if you win?"

"If I win, you get nothing, Skipper. Zero. I go home and I get to choose our next date. How about that?"

Skipper pauses for dramatic effect. Thinking.

"That sounds like a deal."

"Perfect."

"But one question before we start."

"Shoot."

"What alcohol will the shots be?" he asks.

I lick my lips and pull away from him. I love teasing him like that. "Tequila," I say.

He really likes the sound of that. Skipper immediately calls over the waiter and we start the competition.

We get a whole line of shots ready on the table in front of us. Skipper lifts up his first shot and winks at me.

"Ready?" he asks.

"To kick your ass? Always."

We drown our first shot. The alcohol hits me like a wall of fire. I knock it back down my throat.

I may not be a party girl, but I grew up with Cove Finn. I know how to hold my liquor, especially when I had to deal with drinking with my brother for years. I know how to drink a man twice the size of me under the table; I've had plenty of practice.

We both pick up the next shot.

"Ready?" I ask.

"To kick *your* ass? I'm always ready for that, Miss Finn. I can't wait to take you back to my room, then I can *really* spank your ass."

"That's not likely to happen."

BAM. Another shot down.

Things are starting to get a little blurry, but I press on.

Another shot glass in our fingers.

"You still haven't given up?" I ask him, and Skipper shakes his head with a grin.

"Oh, I'm just picturing you naked in my bed, Miss Finn, and it's a very good picture. I'm sure we'll be re-enacting it in a few minutes back at the hotel."

"Not in a million years, Skipper."

BAM. Another shot. Another wall of fire down my throat.

I'm still okay. I'm still okay.

We take another shot. *BAM*. And another. *BAM*.

It's getting tough now.

I'm starting to really feel it.

My body is warm. I want to get out of this dress. I want a shower.

Soon I might even want to throw up.

But I hold it in. I'm not going to give Skipper the satisfaction of taking me home tonight. I'm not going to give in to him that easily.

One more shot.

BAM.

Now my mind is spinning, I feel it in my head. And so does Skipper. He's looking dizzy. If he's that bad, I wonder what I'm looking at. I don't think I can make it past the next shot. I don't think I can do it.

But I still reach forward and grab the next shot glass off the table. The clear tequila looks terrifying to me. This one's gonna destroy me, I know it. I close my eyes and shoot it down.

Ugh. Not good.

I place the empty glass back on the table, and then I realize something. Skipper hasn't taken a glass.

He's shaking his head at me.

He's smiling.

"Fuck me, Sandy, you're too damn good at this," he slurs. "Fine. You win."

I win?

I beat him.

I raise my hand in the air and cheer. Then I immediately lower it.

I feel sick.

I better get home.

My home, not Skipper's hotel room.

I won.

I grab my handbag and stand up from the table whilst Skipper calls over the waiter for the check and places cash down on the table.

"You win, Sandy. I can't take any more."

"Great. So, I get to choose the next date, then."

"There's going to be a next date?"

"If you behave yourself," I reply. "But I'm sick of restaurants and bars. The next date, if it does happen, is gonna be something real."

I wave goodbye to him mockingly and turn to the front doors of Rockpool, feeling quite sick, but also incredibly happy.

Skipper Deep has apologized to me. Skipper Deep really, really wants me. Skipper Deep lost to me in a drinking competition. All in all, that was not too bad of a date.

We'll just have to see if I'm up for a second one.

I step outside and call a taxi home.

12

SKIPPER

I WONDER what the next date will be with Sandy Finn.

Miss Finn, I like saying it like that.

My sexy teacher.

I'm pretty hungover the morning after our so-called not-date.

Fuck me.

Sandy really took it out of me last night. She really screwed me up at that restaurant with that little, but deadly, drinking competition of hers. What was even in those tequila shots, anyway? I'm so hungover this morning that I had to lean over the toilet bowl as soon as I woke up, ready to throw up the entire contents of last night. And I rarely am hungover. It usually takes a lot for me to wake up feeling sick like this and needing a big fry up like the one I've ordered from room service, but that's exactly what Sandy's made me feel when I got out of bed this morning. My bodyguard nearly had a heart attack when he saw me with my pale face and disheveled hair, thinking he'd fucked up his job and I was a goner. I had to reassure him it was merely a hangover before he could freak out too much. Well, technically, Sandy practically did actually *poison* me last night, just with alcohol instead of anything sinister. She really fucked me up, and she knew exactly what she was doing.

That little witch.

Yep, she really knew what she was doing.

She was a beast at drowning those shots. I bet she's had a lot of practice with Cove. Sneaky girl. She really wanted to prove something to me last night. The entire time she was so damn sexy and confident and competitive.

It only makes me want her more.

Yeah, and I apologized to her. It was truthful. From my heart. I am not a sentimental guy; I rarely show my emotions. In my line of work, you've got to stay masculine. Composed. Stoic. Showing what I feel doesn't come naturally to me, but I still let my guard down for Sandy. I showed her what I really felt. I exposed myself to her.

And it was terrifying.

But it needed to be done. I wanted her to see how sorry I am. How the memory of that house party and what I did really has been eating away at my soul every day of my life.

Which just leaves me to wonder, what will our next date be?

It's gonna be something real.

That's what she said.

If she even asks me out again.

Oh, but I think she will.

The thought of her waving mockingly at me as she left the restaurant last night makes me smile. The image of her makes me feel instantly better.

Sandy Finn, I'm out to get you.

I drive up to the school in my Lamborghini and park in

the staff parking lot. I know I shouldn't, but I'm a billionaire. What are they gonna do?

I can do the fuck I want.

Except secure Sandy for a second date, it seems.

I step into the school.

Still wearing my sunglasses. I know my eyes are red from all the drinking. I had two showers and brushed my teeth three times this morning, but I still can't get the goddamn taste of tequila out of my mouth. Sandy really screwed me around last night, but I love it.

I wander down the school hallways. Kids stream in and out of classes. The new school day is starting.

It's good that I'm back, looking to invest in Poseidon's Academy. The place has gone slightly downhill since I was last here as a teenager, but maybe my family's massive education empire might be able to push it up to the big leagues again. This is what I do best. I just need a bit more research into seeing if the place is viable for our company, to see what the problems are here. It's good Mr. Brown has basically given me free rein of the place. It's been interesting sitting in on the different lessons.

But it's not the main reason I'm here, far from it.

Walking around these familiar hallways from my childhood brings back certain memories. It's been years since I've last set foot in this place, but I remember it all as if it were yesterday. The most striking memories are those with Sandy and the things we used to get up to in here after school hours. The *naughty* things we used to do to each other when there was no one around except for the janitors. The secret kisses. The wandering hands. The moans of pleasure from Sandy. All those erotic memories flood into me, even while I'm hungover.

It makes me hungry. It makes me want to taste Sandy Finn again.

She's the main reason I'm back.

And there she is. I see her. Not Sandy, but the other person I've come into school today to see.

"Miss Tweed!" I shout down the hallway at the small figure. Her puffy hair shakes as she turns around. I stroll up to her before she has a chance to react. "You're exactly who I'm looking for."

She blushes at my comment. "Mr. Deep? What a nice surprise to see you."

"Are you free?"

"Right now?"

"Yes."

"Well, I don't have a class for forty-five minutes."

I smile my winning smile at her. I'll charm her little socks off. "Perfect," I say. "I would like to ask you a favor. Nice cardigan, by the way." I nod at her top.

She straightens out her cardigan. "Oh, this old thing. Thank you, Mr. Deep. What can I do for you?"

"I know it's a big ask, but I would like to have a peek at the financial information about the school."

Miss Tweed shakes her head sadly. "Oh, no. That simply isn't possible."

"Why not?"

"Well, Mr. Brown would have to give me authorization first."

I smile again. "Oh, Miss Tweed. I thought you were the school's bookkeeper."

"I am."

"But?"

"But I need Mr. Brown's authorization before I show anyone the financial records, especially someone from outside the school."

"Not just a little peek?" I ask. "How about you stay with me every step of the way?"

"I don't know."

"Think of it as quality time with me. I'd like to get to know you better."

"I really don't think I can."

"You know what? I loved your pearl necklace at the fundraiser. Yesterday, when I was in town, I passed by the jewelry shop and saw this in the window display." I take out a little box from my pocket. I open it up to reveal a shiny silver necklace. It cost me a heck of a lot of money, but I knew I'd need it for this moment. "I saw this in that display and immediately thought of you. I want you to have it."

Miss Tweed blushes again and eyes the necklace greedily. "Oh, Mr. Deep, you're too kind."

"Try it on," I say, enticingly taking the necklace out of the box. Flashing the silver. Miss Tweed eagerly leans her head forward so that I can wrap it around her neck. She really wants it. Perfect. "Wow, Miss Tweed. Fantastic. It really suits you."

"You think?"

"I do."

She pats my chest. I know she just wants to feel my muscular pecs, but I let her. Gotta give her something in return for what I'm asking. "Oh, go on then. I do accept bribes, especially when they come from handsome men. Just a quick peek at those financial records, okay?"

"Yes please, Miss Tweed."

"Follow me."

Yes. That worked. An expensive plan, but it worked.

Miss Tweed leads me down the hallway and into her office. I've not been in here before. She keeps it very secure. The door is locked, and the only keys are hers.

I don't want to judge, but her office is decorated badly. The place is a bit of a mess. Folders and documents everywhere. Tacky photos of meaningless inspirational quotes hang on the walls. The place reeks of her overpowering cheap perfume.

Miss Tweed goes to work gathering all the financial and tax documents. "So," she says as she shifts through her mess. "How's your appraisal of the school going? What do you think of the place?"

"I still need more time," I reply. "It's good so far, but I need some more information."

"More than just the tax records?"

"I need more information from someone who knows everything about the school."

"Oh?"

"You, Miss Tweed. I'm talking about you."

She stops shuffling papers and blinks. "Me?"

"I would like to know your opinion. About what you think of the school," I say. "What would you do or change if you were placed in charge?"

Miss Tweed smiles. She likes this question, I can tell. She likes to imagine being in charge. "Well, there are too many things I would change for a start," she says. "But I'd first like to make some hiring and firing decisions."

"Oh, really?"

She continues to gather the tax and financial documents as she talks. "As I told you the other night at the fundraiser, there's a few people I'd like to let go first. That Miss Finn you spoke to. She'll be the first to go."

"The English teacher?"

"Exactly."

"Interesting."

"She's someone I'd get rid of first. It seems like Poseidon's Academy hired her to bring in some good donations from her family, but she hasn't brought in a penny. She's rude and inconsiderate towards me and my authority as her senior, so she'll have to go. I've had my eye on her for some time. I've been watching her. She's very suspicious."

"I see."

"Here's everything," she says, gesturing at the pile of papers in front of her. "It's all there. Everything for the last five years when I took over."

I walk up to her desk and take a hold of the papers. I smile at her. "You wouldn't mind if I photocopy these, would you?"

13

SKIPPER

THE BELL RINGS, meaning a new class is about to begin.

That's my cue. My chance.

Here we go.

I sprint down the school hallway, avoiding students left, right, and center. I'm holding the gift in my hand, the gift meant for *her*.

"Hey!" One of the kids yells at me as I duck past him, barely missing him as I rush past down the hallway. I don't care about any student who gets in my way, this is my moment.

I turn a corner and there she is.

Sandy Finn.

She's standing outside the door to her classroom, welcoming her English class in. She's greeting each one as they walk through the doorway. She's all smiles. I can see she loves this job. She really does. It makes me go all mushy inside.

Ugh. Emotions.

"Miss Finn," I call out as I turn the corner. I hide the gift behind my back before she can notice it. She lifts her head up. Her eyes are sparkling blue. Gorgeous. Her face is tanned and her hair just perfect. She's my ideal woman. She's worth flying across the world for.

She's worth me coming back to this town.

"Hey," she says. She doesn't seem as pleased to see me as I am to see her. No matter.

I'm going to change that.

"Last night really fucked me over," I say, coming to a stop in front of her.

"No swearing in school."

"Oh, right, Miss Finn."

"Please, just call me Sandy."

"Well, last night really *screwed* me over," I say, emphasis on the not-swear word. She wants to laugh, but she hides it. I can see it, though.

She, unlike me, doesn't seem affected at all by the numerous shots of tequila last night. She looks radiant. An angel.

I really fell into her trap last night, didn't I?

"I'm glad that it did... screw you over."

"Oh, so that's how it is? You're glad you made me wake up with a raging hangover, huh?"

"I don't have time to talk to you now, Skipper," she says, starting to turn inside her classroom. "I have Romeo and Juliet to teach."

"Hang on one second," I reply. I bring out my hand from behind my back, the hand carrying my gift, and show it to her. It's a shiny red apple.

"What's this?"

"It's an apple."

"I know what it is, Skipper. Why are you bringing it to me?"

"You know, the cliché. Bring an apple for the teacher and all that."

Sandy rolls her eyes and shakes her head. She really wants to laugh, and now she's really having to hold it in. She doesn't want to give me the satisfaction of laughing at my stupid joke. It's cute. "I really have to go in now. Nice chatting, Skipper."

I reach out and take her hand before she gets the chance to head inside the classroom. "What about that date?" I ask.

"What date?"

"The date you promised me."

She huffs. "I didn't promise you anything, least of all a date."

"Don't play games with me, Miss Finn. You won that stupid drinking competition last night, so you get to choose what our next date's going to be."

"I didn't promise you one, though," she says with a smirk. She likes teasing me. "I just said I'll choose what the next one would be if it did happen. I get to choose if one *does* happen."

I sigh. She's hard to bargain with, and that's why I like her. Tough as nails. She likes a fight, and I'm gonna give her one. "Well, what would it be if you did choose and if it did happen?" I ask.

"Fine," she replies. "Wait here."

She disappears inside the classroom for a moment. I can't see what she's doing. I wait outside in the hallway like a doofus, hands in my suit pockets. I wonder if she's even going to come back when she reappears at the doorway. She pushes a piece of paper in my hand.

A detention slip.

A piece of paper you give to a misbehaving student with the time and place for an after-school detention. *Great.*

"Does this mean I've been naughty, Miss Finn?" I ask her. "Does this mean I'm in trouble?"

Sandy doesn't reply. She turns around and heads back into the classroom. I swear I see a hint of a grin on her face as she turns.

When she's gone inside, I look down at my hand, down at the detention slip.

It has her handwriting on it. A set of coordinates and a message written in cursive.

Meet me here after school today. For detention. Be on best behavior.

Miss Finn

Oh, the cheeky girl. Alright, I'll play your sneaky games.

As I head back down the hallway, I do a little dance, and I don't care who sees. I know I've got her.

14

SKIPPER

Sandy's waiting there at the beach when I arrive. I park my car next to hers and get out, taking in the view over the clear blue water and raging waves. Below the parking lot, the golden sand of the beach stretches on for miles around.

Sandy leans against her car, sunglasses on and wearing a wetsuit.

A wetsuit?

Wait, we're actually going into the water?

I've rocked up in a suit. I had to input the coordinates she wrote for me on that detention slip into my phone, and when it came up with the beach's location, I knew something was up. She did say that she wanted the next date to be something *real*.

I just didn't know what she truly meant by that, but I get it now.

The beach is definitely something real.

I did pack a pair of swimmers, just in case. Seeing

Sandy in that wetsuit means I'll probably actually have to get them on.

She fits the wetsuit really damn well. It emphasizes her body. Her perky tits. Her round ass. I feel myself get hard at the sight of her leaning against her car. She looks Australian like that. Blonde hair. Tanned skin. My dream girl.

"The beach?" I shout at her over the sound of the roaring waves when I get out of the car.

Sandy bites her lip in excitement. God, that turns me on. "You ready for something real, Skipper?"

"What is this, a swimming competition in the open water?"

"Oh, no. Not that," she says as she pulls herself off the car and opens up the back door. She pulls out something long and white. A surfboard. "This is surfing."

"Surfing?"

She carries the surfboard over to me and thrusts it into my hands. I look down at it in shock. "Yeah, Skipper. Take it."

"I didn't know you surfed."

"When you have such a famous pro surfer like Cove Finn as your brother, then you have to learn how to move on a board pretty quickly," she replies, running her fingers seductively over the surfboard.

"When you said something *real*, I was imagining something more to do with champagne and roses and a hotel suite, not the beach. Not this."

"I'm glad to have tricked you."

"You sly devil. We can always go back to mine and have that champagne and roses."

"Nope."

"Seriously?"

"You ready for some surfing, tough boy, or are you just too scared?"

"Of course, I'm not scared," I reply. "I just haven't surfed in, like, years. Since I was a teenager."

"How about you try it out again? Don't worry, I'm here to hold your hand." She mockingly grabs my hand with hers and I shove it away.

"Get off."

"Aw, don't be so nervous. It's only surfing."

"Right," I say, resting the board against my car. "And what if I don't have a wetsuit?"

Sandy bites her lip again. I'm so, *so* turned on by that. I have to hold myself back from reaching down and kissing her right here and now. "That'll be no problem," she replies. "I stole one of my brother's. He has plenty to spare. I'm sure it'll be the right size for you, you're both tall and muscular."

"Right."

"And," she flicks her sunglasses down her nose, revealing her bright blue eyes. She winks at me. "I've sized you up. I think I know your dimensions."

"Great."

She disappears inside the car for a moment. I lean forward to get a good glimpse of her ass perked in the air as she scrambles inside her car for her brother's spare wetsuit. It's perfectly round. Juicy. I would love to give her a firm spanking. Punish her for her mocking tone towards me this afternoon. She pulls out a wetsuit and throws it at me.

"Put it on."

I look around the beach parking lot. There are a few people around. Some surfers. Some families enjoying the sun after a day in school. I need to strip myself of the suit and change into my swimmers, but I don't want to be exposed to any passers-by.

"I need to get naked," I say, and Sandy laughs.

"Of course. Get to the back of the car and I'll shield you from everyone with a beach towel." I roll my eyes at her suggestion, but she immediately goes to grab a towel. I find my swimmers. Holding both of them and my wetsuit, I stand around at the back of my car, where there are fewer people to view me.

Sandy approaches me holding out a large beach towel spread out so that she's acting like a barrier between me and the parking lot.

"Okay," she says with a cheeky smile. "Get naked."

Oh, she's enjoying this.

I point at the towel. "With just that covering me?"

"Yep. Go ahead."

A date doing something real?

More like a date spent embarrassing me in every way.

She wants to shame me. She wants to have the upper hand over me. And, if I truly want her in the way that I do, I'll have to play along.

Oh, she's a clever girl.

"You're gonna watch?" I ask cheekily.

"I'm not planning to," she replies, turning her head away from me exaggeratedly. "There isn't much to see, anyway."

"Hang on."

"Just hurry up and get naked, Skipper."

I turn around towards the car so that, if she did peek, she'd only see my ass. My perfectly toned ass. I start unbuttoning my suit. Then I remove my jacket. Then I pull down my pants.

I'm completely naked.

I quickly turn my head around.

Just as I expect, Sandy is watching me. Scanning my muscular body. Checking out my toned ass.

I smile and turn around so that she can see *everything*.

My long manhood that hangs free and loose between my legs.

"Satisfied with what you see?" I ask. I place my hands on my hips.

If she's going to get me naked in public to humiliate me, then I'm going to make her see everything. That's what she really wants.

Sandy's cheeks flush red, but she doesn't take her eyes off me.

"Eh, you've shrunk since I last saw you," she says with a smile.

Oh, damn.

"So, this is how it's going to be?"

I bend over and pull up my swimmers and the wetsuit, covering up my exposed naked body. Disappointing Sandy.

"Right," I say. "Let's surf."

We take the two boards down to the beach. Standing there, in front of the crashing tall waves, I'm really reminded of how I hadn't been on one of those things since I was last in this small town as a teenager. It's been a long, long time. I turn to Sandy and she's smiling. She loves this, and I'm not going to give her the pleasure of knowing how nervous I am.

She makes me nervous in ways I've never felt. Even with all the high-powered business meetings and negotiations over millions of dollars, I've never felt as nervous as when I do around Sandy Finn. She has a hold over me that's like no other.

We take the boards and dive into the cold water. We start paddling out, the two of us side-by-side. Sandy laughs all the way, an infectious laugh. A laugh that makes me fancy her even more.

We paddle out far, then sit on the boards together, waiting for a suitable wave.

"I've heard you've got exams coming up?" I ask.

"Yeah, the whole school does," she replies. "They're super important. Each class receives an average mark and then we get compared with all the different departments."

"Are you nervous about it?"

Sandy nods. "Yeah. There are two boys in my class I'm most worried about. James and Tom. They like to fight. Muck up. It's pretty difficult wasting time making sure they're not being naughty *and* trying to teach a class of twenty others about Shakespeare."

"Sounds tough."

"It is." We see a pack of waves emerging. Perfect. "Here they come."

I catch the first wave to come. The board nearly flies out from under my body, but I manage to keep a hold of it. I shoot down the wave. My old teenage self kicks in and I push myself up on the board.

I'm standing.

I bend my knees and balance myself. I've got to stay focused. I don't want to fall off early. I'm too competitive in life and in surfing to allow that to happen. I'm sure Sandy would love me to embarrass myself on the board. She'll love to rub it in.

I ride the board into shore.

Yes.

I did it. I surfed.

I spin around to catch Sandy smiling at me.

"How's that for something real?" I ask, and Sandy pokes her tongue out at me.

After our surfing session, we head back up to the parking lot and our cars. I strip down so that I'm only wearing my swimmers and I hand Cove's spare wetsuit over to Sandy.

"Thanks," she says. We're standing together by my car.

I'm in just my swimmers. My muscular upper body is dripping wet. Sandy's blonde hair is damp in a sexy beach way.
There's an electricity in the air between us, it's like we don't
want the other to leave. Like we're waiting for something.
There's a spark between us.

"No, thank you," I reply. "For this unusual date.
It *was* something real, after all."

She takes a step towards me and I take a step towards
her.

I lean over her face. Her mouth's already waiting for
mine like she's asking a question. I find her lips and lightly
touch them with my own. Her soft, cherry lips open up to
me. Her eyes close.

And then we are kissing.

She tastes of the sun and the ocean. I drink her in. Enve-
lope her.

I miss this. I miss her touch. Her taste.

This is what I've been craving for all these years.

I feel her defenses slowly melt away until she's kissing
me back. She wants to put up a wall between us, but knows
it's not right. She knows what she truly feels, and that's
kissing me back. And she does.

This is natural. This is what both of us want.

My hands fit around her body and I'm pulling her in
under my arms. Our kiss becomes stronger until it's like
we're clawing at each other's mouths. We want each other
so badly. We're both wild and out of control. She wants me
as much as I want her.

Eight years apart can make you so hungry for the other
person.

This is so right.

We don't let go of each other for minutes, and it feels
like an eternity. A glorious eternity. And when we finally
do let go, it's like we're trying to breathe again. We've been

overpowered by the other so much we forgot to bring in air.

We're silent for a moment after our lips separate. I stare into her blue eyes and she stares back at mine.

I smile.

Her arms let go of mine, and I feel her slipping away.

"That was a mistake," she says, softly.

"What?"

"I can't forget about the past. That night."

"Oh." And it's like a thousand daggers are penetrating my heart. That night. That stupid house party. I wish I could take it all back. I wish I never did what I've done. I will hate myself for that night for the rest of my life.

I'll never be let go for that one awful mistake.

Sandy faces the ground and steps back.

"I can never go home with you, Skipper."

And that sentence destroys me. Even though I know, in her heart, it's not true. I felt her during that kiss. She wants me as much as I want her. I know that. She knows that. She's just so scared, and I understand why.

Me.

She's afraid of me.

She's afraid of what I did to her eight years ago. She doesn't want her heart broken like that again.

And who can blame her?

"What can I say?" I ask. "I will never do what I did eight years ago again to you. I made a terrible mistake then, and I will never repeat it. Never."

There's a long pause. Sandy's thinking it over.

"You promise?"

I take in a deep breath. This is serious. This is real. She's asking me from the depths of her soul; this isn't a promise to take lightly. This is as important as it gets. "I promise."

Sandy takes another moment to take my words in.

Then she shakes her head, and I know it's all over.

"I can't..."

"Why?"

"I can't do this."

She ducks her head and jumps into her car. She quickly turns on the ignition and drives away, leaving me alone at the beach.

I watch her car disappear into the distance.

I know she wants me. I know she needs me. I saw the hesitation in her eyes. I tasted the doubt on her lips.

I'll fight for her love.

15

SANDY

THAT KISS.

That stupid, glorious kiss.

I couldn't stop thinking about it all night. One moment I was sure it was a mistake, another big mistake I've made, but then the next moment I was sure it was the best thing that's ever happened to me.

Was it good? Or was it bad?

Was it right I kissed him, or a sign of weakness?

Should I have let him?

And on and on cycled my thoughts all night, flipping from one extreme to the other. Keeping me awake until dawn, until sunlight flooded my bedroom.

Skipper Deep, once again, dominating my mind.

I know one thing for sure: I fell into that kiss. I wanted it and I loved it and hated it at the same time. I couldn't hold myself back from reaching out and touching Skipper's lips at that parking lot, even if I tried not to. I felt his lips so hard against mine that I just had to give in. I shouldn't blame myself. Little shivers of pleasure, shock, doubt, and panic shot through my body all together at the same time as we touched. A strange cocktail of both knowing how much of a mistake I was making and also overwhelming pure desire for the beautiful man wrapping his lips around mine. There was something in the air between us as we kissed, some kind of power that I couldn't resist.

I couldn't resist him.

I didn't know what to do with myself when I drove home after that kiss. Sure, I told him I couldn't trust him and that I couldn't do that again, but at the same time, I still felt my heart back at that beach with him, unable to let go. What did I expect to happen when I invited him on a second date? What did I want?

I wanted him.

But I still couldn't get over that night eight years ago.

All the way home, my mind was in a tumble. I couldn't think straight.

Images of Skipper and his naked body filled my mind. The way he smiled at me when he was fully exposed to me at the beach. The desire I felt within me, that warmth that grew inside my body when I saw his naked body again.

So pent up with energy, I went home and did what any self-respecting woman would do in these circumstances.

I made myself a hot bath.

I needed to relax, release the frantic nerves within me.

Calm myself.

Quiet the raging thoughts going through my head.

I needed to get out of the past. Stop living in it. Stop thinking of Skipper as that stupid teenage boy eight years ago.

He was different now.

He *promised* to me in that beach parking lot he wouldn't break my heart again.

But could I trust him?

Could I *really*?

I didn't know.

I still don't know, even after that hot bath. My mind is still a mess.

I don't know what to think anymore; everything's up in the air. Nothing makes sense. I've already been on two dates with the man who I told myself I would never see again. I am already falling for his charm all over again.

I made myself a hot bath and melted into it, closing my eyes and dreaming of Skipper and his naked body.

And then I spent a night tossing and turning in bed, unable to sleep. Unable to decide whether that kiss had been the biggest mistake, or the best moment, of my life.

And now a new day. A new school day.

I'm unrested. Wound up. My head's scrambled.

Because of him.

And I've just received an email from Mr. Brown summoning me to his office immediately after school.

Shit. Not good.

And, to top it all off, my English class was a mess. Again. It didn't help that my mind was in twenty different places at once. I couldn't control the students.

Tom and James were at it again. Fighting. Yelling at each other. Those two boys were like little demons. They hated my class more than they hated each other, which was saying a lot. It was like they were out to get me. It only worked when I sent Tom outside to sit alone in the school hallway and kept James inside away from each other. I had to spend the entire class using all my energy keeping them apart and not on actually teaching Romeo and Juliet to the rest of my students.

Am I failing as a teacher?

Was Miss Tweed right?

Am I just a poor excuse for an educator?

I really worry about my students' exams. They are all going to fail English and it is going to be all my fault. I'll get sacked, and that'll be my teaching career over. The one thing that gives me joy, gone.

I'll be left with nothing, all alone in my empty house.

No career. No goals. No life.

After my class of the day, I head across the school to the principal's office. I don't feel up to this meeting, whatever it is. I just need to sleep. And, most of all, I need to get Skipper Deep out of my mind.

I knock on the principal's door and I hear Mr. Brown's voice calling me to open.

Inside the office is Mr. Brown sitting behind his desk and, standing next to him, is Miss Tweed.

Shit, shit, shit.

This really can't be good.

Miss Tweed glares at me as I step into the office, a smug smirk on her face.

Yeah, whatever this is, it can't be good.

"Uh, hello Mr. Brown," I say. "You wanted to see me?"

"Yes, Miss Finn. Please, sit down."

I do so at his desk. Miss Tweed stands over me, still smiling.

"What's this about?" I ask.

Mr. Brown leans back in his chair. "How's everything going, Miss Finn?"

"Good. Everything's good. The students are starting to get stuck into Shakespeare. We're making good progress."

"Excellent, and what do you think of the exams? Do you think they'll go well?"

"I hope so. With enough hours and enough study time, I think I can get the students up to speed and confident about the exams."

"And how is it with Mr. Deep?" Mr. Brown asks.

The question throws me. I open and close my mouth like a goldfish.

"Skip - *Mr. Deep?* In what way?"

Before Mr. Brown can answer, Miss Tweed interrupts.

"Something is not going right with Mr. Deep," she asserts. "Mr. Deep has not invested in the school yet or has made any indication that he's going to buy shares in this place. I'm getting worried, Miss Finn, especially because it seems like Mr. Deep seems satisfied with everything else in the school. Everything except for you, Sandy."

"What are you talking about?" I ask, indignant. Miss Tweed continues like I haven't spoken.

"I really do hope that you are not going to be the one thing that holds back the school from Mr. Deep's potential large investment."

"I don't believe this," I reply. "I'm not doing anything to stop Mr. Deep."

"You sure?" Miss Tweed asks.

Tears come to my eyes. What is it with this woman and her ability to always make me come to the verge of crying? She's a horrible person. A terrible person. "I just want to teach my class," I say. "I just want to see them do well at their exams. I just want them to develop a love of Shakespeare and English."

It's true.

It's all I care about. My students falling in love with Shakespeare and words and poetry and the English language. That's all that matters here, not some kind of weird school politics with Miss Tweed and fundraisers and money. I'm here for the pure love of teaching.

I turn my attention to Mr. Brown. The nervous man isn't saying anything. He's completely in thrall to Miss Tweed. She's the one holding all the power inside the school, even though she's just another teacher like me. He's weak. He lets her ride all over him.

"I've got my eye on you, Miss Finn," Miss Tweed says. Her face narrows into a scowl.

She hates me.

She wants me gone, out of the school, and she's going to use Skipper as an excuse to do so.

I can't believe this.

"If Mr. Deep doesn't invest," Mr. Brown says. "And your students don't do well in the exams, then I'm afraid we'll have to look at your performance."

"What do you mean?"

Miss Tweed nods. "It means," she says. "That you're going to have to work *extra hard* to not lose your job, okay?"

16

SANDY

I CLOSE the door to Mr. Brown's office and nearly break down in the middle of the school hallway in floods of tears.

How dare Miss Tweed insinuate that I'm holding the school back?

Every day she seems to insult my integrity, my teaching ability, my *passion* for my students and my school. Every single day, she brings me down with her directed attacks. And now, after our little meeting in the principal's office, I can see she's got Mr. Brown on her side; the principal fully believes her and her lies about me.

It's hopeless to resist.

I love this school. I love my students. I love teaching.

I can't get fired.

I wipe my face and start walking with my shoulders back. I'm not going to cry in school again, especially not in its hallways. Not where I can be seen.

The place is empty. There's silence. The students have gone home. There are only the janitors about.

When the place is empty like this, I'm reminded of my days here with Skipper, back when we were teenagers. Sneaking a few kisses in empty classrooms. Playing with each other away from the security cameras.

Those were good days.

And now I'm fighting for my job.

I head back towards my classroom. I have a stack of work to finish and now, in the quiet of the empty school, I can finally get started. Take my mind off the crises I've just been thrown into by the principal and Miss Tweed.

I turn the corner.

What's that?

I hear noises coming from my classroom. The door's open, and voices are echoing from inside.

It's after school; there should be no one there.

But there is. Someone's talking.

I duck up against the wall and listen. Male voices. I inch closer to the open doorway and peek around the corner to get a view of whoever it is.

It's Skipper.

He's in my classroom with his back to the doorway.

What the hell?

What is he playing at? He needs to leave my classroom immediately. I'm going to be so furious when I storm inside.

But before I barge in, I want to listen in on what he's talking about. I think he's in there with other people.

Let me hear for a second. Let me see what he's up to.

It can't be anything good.

"So, let me run this whole play down for you because it's one heck of a thing to understand properly. I understand its difficulties. I had to study it when I was your age. I had to study it with Miss Finn when she was a teenager."

He's talking about me?

He's talking about Shakespeare?

What is he saying? Who is he saying this to?

"What was she like?"

Who's that talking? Sounds young.

A boy.

"What? Miss Finn? She was pretty stuck up. She was a nerd, but, hey, a very pretty one. I basically fell in love with her on sight right then and there."

"Ew!"

Another boy to the one talking earlier.

Who is Skipper talking to?

"Yes, *ew*. Okay, should we go through this stupid play or not?"

There's a murmur of approval.

"Alright," Skipper starts, clearing his throat exaggeratedly. "There are these two families, right, who are basically gangs. They hate each other. There are a lot of fights and violence between them all. One of these gangs has a daughter, the other one has a son, and they meet at a party and instantly fall in love."

"Instantly? Like you and Miss Finn?"

Skipper chuckles. "Yeah, James, kind of."

James? The other boy was Tom?

Wait.

Skipper is talking about Romeo and Juliet to Tom and James? Together? He's *teaching* Shakespeare to the two naughtiest boys in my class who want to kill each other?

No freaking way.

How did he even get them in a room together without fisticuffs? How has he managed to get them to sit in a classroom together?

How has he got them to be calm?

"So, let's go back to the story."

I stand here, in the empty school hallway, overhearing Skipper chat endlessly about Romeo and Juliet in great depth to the two boys who couldn't sit still for a single *moment* in my class. He goes through everything in the play, and he's funny about it. Real funny. He makes them laugh along with him, even me. I can't help but giggle when he breaks down the plot as if it's a modern-day gangster romance.

It's kinda cute. He's kinda cute, and gorgeous, in the way he's chatting about the play. One thing's for sure, he's got their entire attention as he speeds through the plot outline, something I've not managed to do at all. Not with these boys.

I would never have thought in a million years you could get these boys to learn Shakespeare, or even get them in the same room together.

Skipper's a natural teacher.

My heart goes crazy peeking at him teaching James and Tom. He's very adorable in his teacher mode, all gestures and imitating funny accents.

My mind wanders to that kiss yesterday. That strange, strange kiss I can't think straight about. It did feel so natural, but I'm still so angry about his cheating past. But, then again, he's so beautiful talking to these two boys about Romeo and Juliet.

I just don't know what to think. My *heart* doesn't know what to think.

And, just as he reaches the end of describing the play, I decide I've heard enough.

I'm going in.

I take a step inside my classroom and announce myself to the three males.

"What's going on here?"

Tom and James are shocked at my entrance. Their mouths hang open like they've been caught in the act.

Two little troublemakers, for sure.

But, instead of being surprised by my sudden entrance like I'd wanted him to be, Skipper merely slowly turns around and flashes me his trademark cocky smile. Like he knew I'd turn up.

Like he's expecting me.

God, he's so infuriating.

And so handsome.

"Oh, I'm just teaching the boys some Shakespeare. It's fun, isn't it, boys?"

They laugh.

That's his reply?

The cheeky bastard. He knows what he's doing. He knows how much he's annoying me with his little antics here.

"Hi, Tom. Hi, James."

"Hello, Miss Finn," they both say in unison.

The bastard's not getting away with teaching my kids.

"Can I speak to you outside, Skipper?" I ask. "Alone."

"Sure thing." He winks at the boys and spins around, following me into the hallway. I close the classroom door behind him so that my two troublesome students can't hear.

"What's going on here? Why are you teaching my students?"

Skipper chuckles and places his hand on my shoulder. It's annoying, but I make no effort to shrug him off. His face is very close to mine and, despite what I want to do, my body starts to go weak at the knees for him. "You told me on the surfboard yesterday you were having trouble with these two boys, and I thought I might be able to help," he explains with his trademark smile.

"I don't need your help."

"Well," he continues. "Please give me some credit. I've got them sitting down together and talking, and now we're onto Shakespeare. It's a lot more than what you've done."

"A lot more than what I've done?"

He shrugs. "Yeah. I've got James and Tom to chill out and listen. Give me some credit on that, at least."

"They're *my* students."

"They need *my* help."

"Really?" I ask, raising an eyebrow.

"They have the exams coming up and I know how to talk to teenage boys. Look at the progress I've already made in just an hour. They're listening to my every word."

Oh, he's being *really* cheeky now.

"Really?" It's my only comeback I can think of on the spot. I'm sure I'll think of one in bed later when it's much too late. As usual.

Skipper just keeps on smiling. "I can clearly see you're annoyed with me, so how about a deal?"

"A deal?"

"Yeah, and this one isn't a drinking competition."

"Right."

"How about we do this together?"

"Together?"

"You heard me."

"You mean teach the boys together?"

"Yeah. I like them," Skipper says. "And I like you. It sounds like a good deal to me."

This man.

But he is right. He *has* got Tom and James to sit down together and listen. He has been able to explain the whole plot of Romeo and Juliet to them without any fights breaking out. Maybe I do need his sorry ass to help.

What else can I do? I'm probably gonna lose my job in a few weeks, thanks to Miss Tweed.

"You have been good getting them together," I reply.

"Yeah."

"And you do know your Shakespeare."

"Well, I was in the same class as you, so of course you forced me to practically memorize Romeo and Juliet. So, what do you say?"

I eye him suspiciously. He's playing a game here; I know he's only doing this just to spend more time with me. He wants me to accept. He doesn't care that I rejected his kiss yesterday. He *wants* me so much he's prepared to spend time teaching kids about Shakespeare.

And, secretly, deep down, I want him.

Screw it.

"It's a deal," I say.

Skipper takes my hand. His warm touch sends lightning through my body. I hide my little gasp of pleasure from him as he pulls me back inside the classroom. James and Tom are sitting at their desks, watching us carefully.

"Right," Skipper says. "Listen up boys."

"You want to tell them?" I ask him.

"Yes please," he says. The two boys perk up as he speaks. "Miss Finn and I have come to an agreement. Every Monday you two are to stay behind for private lessons with us two. We're gonna teach you Shakespeare. Together. How does that sound?"

17

SKIPPER

"How about another kiss?" I ask Sandy as I close the classroom door.

"No, Skipper."

"You sure?"

"I'm sure, you weirdo."

It's another Monday, another day after school teaching James and Tom about Romeo and Juliet. As I ask Sandy for another kiss, the boys have just left, leaving the teacher and me alone in her classroom together.

And the tension in the air between us is striking.

I can feel it, and I know she can too.

We just have to act upon it.

It's been four weeks since Sandy barged in on me secretly teaching the two teenage tearaways about the basics of Shakespeare in her classroom, and everything's just gone swimmingly from then. Every Monday after school, just as we told them to do, the two teenage boys have stayed behind for us to spend an hour seriously teaching them one-on-one.

Catching them up on what the rest of the class has done. Sandy, although pretty cold to the tutoring idea at the beginning, has really started to warm up to it. We've reached the point now when she's actually laughing along and finally being loose with the play. I think our different teaching styles somehow complement each other. She's more detail-orientated and academic, whilst I'm a bit more fun and relaxed with the boys, able to talk to them man-on-man. I'm never afraid to just use a big metaphor to describe something that I know would otherwise be boring to a teenage boy.

We make a good team.

And, as I can see from her face when she thinks I'm not looking, I know Sandy thinks so too.

Each week the boys get better and better at English. They understand more and more about the play and, at this rate, they're practically gonna be Shakespeare experts.

And it's all down to Sandy and me.

Yeah, Sandy and I make a great team.

Which has led us to this week. We've given the boys a pretty insurmountable task for them to complete. We want them to memorize, and then perform out loud in front of us, the famous Romeo balcony speech.

But, soft, what light through yonder window breaks? It is the East, and Juliet is the sun.

Yeah, that one.

I had to memorize the same speech when I was their age in this very classroom we are sitting in, so I'm sure these boys can, too. Sandy, though, was not so convinced when I ran her past the idea. She told me she didn't think they were up to it already. They weren't prepared. Nonsense, I said. If I could do it at their age, then any boy can. Just you wait and see.

Teaching these boys has allowed Sandy and me to get

even closer. We haven't been on another date since the day we went surfing and *that* kiss. I don't think she's ready for another date so soon, but she's definitely lowered her barriers around me. She's slowly letting me through her walls. I can see every day that she's actually realizing I'm not that stupid boy from eight years ago, that I've come back to New Water as a new man. A man who won't cheat on her like I did back then. A man who can keep his promise to stay with her. I know I just have to give her more time to heal. I know I screwed up her heart badly when I fucked up eight years ago. I know these wounds to the soul take time to heal and I've got to let her do that on her own, whilst I show up every Monday to prove I'm not the same man I was eight years ago.

She actually laughs at my jokes now and touches me on the arm when she likes what I'm saying. We're not awkward around each other anymore. I see her watching me when she thinks I'm not looking. I can see she admires the way I deal with the boys, how I talk to them and teach them. I know she really likes that.

I've just got to give her more time.

And, just to prove her wrong, the boys individually step up in front of us in the classroom and perform the Romeo balcony speech. It's amazing watching them. Sure, they each stumble over some of the words. They're no West End Shakespearean actors. But both of them manage to get through the entire speech. Completely memorized.

I'm pretty goddamn proud.

Sandy is gob smacked. She never knew they had it in them to do this. I did, though. I watch her as each boy speaks the speech. She's so *overjoyed* at what the boys are accomplishing. I'm glad to have given her this.

We congratulate the two boys with a round of enthusiastic applause from both of us. They beam at us, happy to make us proud. A few weeks ago, you couldn't put James and Tom in the same classroom without fear of them punching each other up, but now they're actually friends and are reciting actual Shakespeare.

Not too bad for a guy who's not a qualified teacher.

And then, applause over, I hand over the online video game store vouches I promised them and told them to get out of here.

Tom and James leave the classroom, excited to have the vouchers to spend. I close the door behind them and then jokingly ask for a kiss from Sandy. She's sitting on one of her students' tables in the middle of the room.

I don't think she's happy.

"Come on," I say. "Just another kiss?"

"No."

"Well, can't say I didn't try," I reply. "Pretty good about their speeches, hey?"

I do a little celebratory dance on the spot. Yeah, it's goofy, but I'm trying to amuse Sandy.

But she's not amused. She doesn't laugh at my silly dance. Instead, she's staring at me, her eyes narrowed suspiciously. Her voice is low and accusatory. "Skipper, tell me one thing."

"What?"

"Tell me, did you promise Tom and James you'd give them video game vouchers if they memorized that speech?"

I shrug. "Yeah. Why not?"

Ah, I thought she'd be pissed off about that.

Sandy shakes her head. "You can't bribe kids, Skipper. Especially not with vouchers."

"Why not?"

"Because we're teachers," she splutters out in disbelief. "We can't just do that."

I smile and shrug. "I'm not a teacher though," I reply. "I can bribe them with whatever I like."

Sandy shakes her head again and starts to laugh. She can't hold it in. "You're such an idiot, Skipper."

"That bribe got them to do it, didn't it? It got them to memorize Shakespeare."

Even Sandy can't find fault with my logic. She sighs in exasperation. "Yeah, it did," she admits.

"So," I flirt, strolling towards her. "I count that as a win."

"You think you're so cool for getting them to memorize that speech even after I said they couldn't? You think you're so cool that you can bribe teenage boys into learning, don't you?"

I nod. "Yeah, pretty much," I reply, flicking my hair back nonchalantly. I sit down on the table next to hers, my legs swinging. "I think I'm pretty cool, and even you have to admit, I'll make a great teacher."

"No, you wouldn't."

"Yes, I would."

"No, you so wouldn't, and even if your students did pass the exams, it'll only be because you bribed each of them with a new car."

"Maybe. If it works," I reply. I flick my hand around the room. "Remember when we used to be in this classroom at their age?"

Sandy lowers her face and smiles. She's blushing. "Yeah, this same classroom. It's so strange. Doesn't it feel like a million years ago?"

I lean over and take her hand, pulling her to her feet. I stand up as well.

"Remember back in those days when we would sneak in here after school, just like now?"

"Of course," she replies with a nervous smile.

"We would make out passionately in here and always

be super worried about the janitor bursting in. We'd always been on the lookout for his footsteps approaching."

Sandy takes a step back so that she's up against the wall. "You mean before you slept with my best friend?"

Oh, she's tough.

"Remember how we did some pretty crazy things in here? Some wild things in here after school?"

Sandy bits her lower lip. Her eyes scan my body up and down. She leans back against the wall, and I know she's remembering how I used to touch her in here. I am. The way my hands could make her whole body shake. Yeah, she remembers that, well, at least her pussy does. "Oh, Skipper, I've *completely* forgotten what you're talking about. What wild things did we used to do in here? Remind me."

She's breathless, lost in the fantasy, and so am I. Those things we used to do in here, I want to repeat them now. Under my suit, my cock is hard, and her body is hot so close to mine.

I want to fuck her so bad.

This is my cue. I take a step forward so that we're so close. I practically have her pinned against the wall, but Sandy loves it. Her breathing is fast and shallow. Her pupils are dilated. Her cheeks flushed. She slowly parts her lips open and leans towards me like she wants to drink me in. Like she's inhaling me. I lift my arms up and pin her hands against the wall. She doesn't struggle against my grip.

She wants this.

She wants me.

Fucking finally.

"Crazy things like this," I whisper as my face inches closer to hers. Her full lips are wet; I can almost taste them.

Our lips meet. Our faces collide.

And then we're kissing.

18

SANDY

SKIPPER KISSES ME.

And I kiss back.

His mouth is soft against mine, but he's so hungry for me. He tastes sweet. His designer stubble scratches against my chin, but I love the rough feel against my skin. I love how it makes me fully understand I'm kissing a real man. They say that kissing feels like melting, and with Skipper Deep, it really does. My body collapses into his muscular frame. His strength makes me go weak. I give in to him and his commanding power.

I can't hold myself back any longer.

His fingers are wrapped tightly around my wrists above my head. He has me pinned up against the wall. He has control and I don't fight back.

I don't want to fight back.

He can have me totally.

I let him do what he wishes. I want him to ravage me

like this. I want him to feel dominant. I want to give him what he desires. I want this. I want him.

I let go of everything, all my doubts and fears, and just let Skipper's lips press up against mine. My fears of his cheating past evaporate from my thoughts as I feel his tongue enter my willing mouth. I no longer doubt if he says who he is when I suck on him, biting his full lip on a passionate impulse. A wave of pleasure rushes through me. All my barriers to him are down now. Lost. I'm completely his.

He lets go of me and I feel his hands brush tenderly down my arms. My skin prickles at his touch. His fingers flow down the curves of my body to come to rest on my waist, completely ignoring my breasts. His teasing sends me into orgasmic agony. I wanted him to hold my tits. I dig my own fingers into his chest in annoyance. He knew what he was doing. The pressure has built up for too long. The tension is too strong for me to ignore it anymore. I can't stand it any further. It needs to come out.

"I want you to fuck me," I whisper between kisses. Skipper doesn't stop moving. He doesn't register what I've said except for when I feel his lips turn out into a wicked smile. It's like he *knew* I would find him irresistible. Like he was just *waiting* for me to give into him. He's so annoying, but so clever and gorgeous. I just can't simply resist him. I mean, how could I even resist that perfect jawline?

I groan.

"Let's do what we used to do as teenagers," he says to me. Well, it's more like he *commands* me, and I am more than willing to obey him. "Let me remind you what wild things we used to get up to in here, in this classroom."

I know what he wants.

"Give yourself to me, you naughty boy," I tease.

Skipper hisses as I kneel down in front of him and start

reaching desperately for the zipper to his suit. I quickly tear it down and dig my hand inside. I don't have to search for long before I find that long cock I've been fantasizing about since seeing it again in full, exposed view at the beach a few weeks ago. Man, I've missed this long shaft.

I pull Skipper's hard dick from his pants. He's completely erect. So long and thick. Just what I need.

Just what I've missed.

Skipper groans as I begin to lick the head of his cock. I begin to make out with it, tasting it, nibbling at it. Skipper groans again. Oh, I love teasing him like this. I can see the desire in his eyes like flames, the way he looks at me with such an intense glare. He wants me to wrap my cherry lips around his cock. Okay, I'll obey. I place the whole thing into my open mouth, gagging on it. Welcoming it in. His hands run through my hair. He simply can't get enough of me, nor I him. I suck on his thick cock. This is just like what we used to do as teenagers. Skipper would pin me in these empty dark classrooms and fuck my mouth. I taste his cock in my mouth; that familiar length fills me with delight. I moan again, gagging on his long dick.

And then I let go. His member falls out of my mouth and I smile up at Skipper. He looks shocked that I've pushed him so far just to stop.

"You like that?" I ask with my sultry voice. Skipper just nods. "You like that?"

Yeah, he does like that.

Teasing him turns me on, makes me wet. I'm aroused.

Skipper's hands find mine and he's lifted me back on my feet. His hands are all over my body, ripping off my clothes. I let him take control and undress me. His desire for me is overpowering. He wants me and isn't afraid to rip off my clothes to get me.

"You've been a bad, bad girl, Miss Finn," Skipper groans. "Teasing me like this. Very bad indeed."

"Mhm, what are you gonna do about it?"

"I'm going to punish you."

It's just my bra and panties left on. Skipper spins me around and forces me down onto one of the desks, pinning me to it. I moan.

Yep, he can do whatever he wants with me.

He unclips my bra as I feel his stubble travel down my body to between my legs. His mouth is heading towards my pussy. I'm so wet for him that I moan in unbearable anticipation. His hands tear aside my panties as his mouth makes contact with my sex. His wet tongue slides up me, teasing me, making me moan again. It's like my body's on fire like he's setting me on flames with his mouth. I arch my back on the desk and moan once more.

"Don't stop, Skipper," I grunt through gasps. "Don't you dare stop this."

And he doesn't.

He presses his mouth in deeper and I feel his tongue delicately flick over my clit. My body squirms. I pull against his strong grip. His hands are around my thighs, holding onto me with such force. My knees wrap around his perfect head and I push into his mouth. He takes me completely. His tongue finds places I don't know exist and I'm launched into orgasmic joy.

"I want you inside me," I whisper, breathless. "I need you inside me. I need you to fuck me."

"I've been dreaming about this for so long," he says.

"Me too," I reply. "I've woken up thinking of you, being *wet* for you."

"And did you touch yourself?"

"Yes."

"Thinking of me?"

"Yes."

"You naughty girl, you really need to be punished for those bad thoughts."

And then he's standing, tearing open a condom packet.

"I'm going to fuck you so hard," he says with that intense gaze of unfiltered desire in his eyes. "I'm going to use you, Sandy. I'm going to fuck you."

And he does. His cock enters me, and I go wild. My eyes roll back, and my body screams in pleasure. My heart thuds in my chest as he pounds into me, thrusting with enough strength I'm worried about breaking in half. But I don't, and Skipper continues to fuck me with all his physical force. Our eyes meet and then he leans over and is kissing me in one quick move. He takes my lower lip between his teeth and hangs on as he thrusts over and over into me again until he starts to shake.

His cock inside my twitches and he unloads, calling out my name in a grunt as he does so.

"Sandy."

I moan as he collapses on top of me, panting.

Fuck me.

That was incredible.

I can hardly breathe.

"You really forgot about this?" Skipper whispers into my ear.

I shake my head. "How could I ever forget about this?"

19

SANDY

SKIPPER COVERS my mouth and hushes me quiet.

"Wait," he whispers. "Can you hear that?"

His warm palm still covers my mouth. It would be kind of comical if I were looking at this situation from an outsider's perspective. We're both half-dressed, standing in my school classroom with Skipper holding me quiet with his palm. I want to laugh, but Skipper doesn't find it funny, even though his pants are tied around his knees.

We wait a few moments. Skipper closes his eyes, intently listening.

Nothing.

No sound.

He sighs and lets go of my mouth.

"Why did you do that for?" I ask, bending over to continue dressing myself. He was being pretty rude.

Skipper shrugs. "I thought I heard somebody outside the door. The janitor, I think. But clearly not."

I snort. "The janitor?"

"Yeah."

"What are you, fifteen again? Scared of the janitors, are we, Mr. Deep? Not such a big business boy now."

He wiggles an accusatory finger at me. "Don't you laugh. You wouldn't like it if we were caught."

I start properly laughing then. His serious face combined with the fact his pants are still needed to be pulled up is such a funny sight. "A billionaire who's over six feet tall is scared of a janitor seeing him half-naked."

"Well, I don't want anyone barging into this classroom post-sex. It's a perfectly logical fear."

"You're such a baby, Skipper," I say, covering my mouth to stop me spitting; I'm laughing so much.

"Okay, okay," he replies. "It isn't *that* funny."

"No," I say. "It is."

"Shut up."

"Look at us both," I say. "We're acting like teenagers. Scared of the janitor. Having secret sex in the classroom. It's really like we've de-aged eight years."

"Well, that's not too bad. I liked being a teenager, especially when it came to fucking you."

"You've got a dirty mind, Mr. Deep."

Skipper sits down on a chair and fits his shoes back on. He flicks his gorgeous hair back. "But, seriously though," he says, locking eyes with me. "I've only thought of you."

I roll my eyes. "Yeah, I bet you say that to all the women."

"No, *seriously*. Yeah, I've been around. I've been around quite a lot, but all I've ever thought about was you."

My heart begins to race, and I can't think straight. Is he actually telling the truth here? Is this really how strong he thinks about me?

"Don't you lie to me, Skipper. Don't you dare. Not about this."

He raises his hands. I don't know if he's still being funny, or if he's actually deadly serious. "I'm not lying. It's true. No one has ever compared to you. There's a place in my heart that's all yours and no one's been able to pierce it since. How many times can I tell you that I know it's a mistake what I did to you?"

"Maybe a few more thousand. That'll be right. Yeah, that will make it right."

Skipper sighs. "So, how about you? Have you been thinking of me for the last eight years?" he asks.

I tilt my head at him. "What do you think?"

"I don't know."

I'm not going to let down my guard that easily.

"Well, at least you're back," I say. And it's true. I'm happy he's back. I can admit that to myself now. I'm happy to see him again, kiss him again, make love to him again.

"Yeah," Skipper replies with his goofy smile. "Now I'm back."

20

SANDY

I TAKE off in my car and head straight to the beach. Parking, I jump out of the vehicle and walk down the stairs into the sand. I sit overlooking the water and stare out into the horizon. There are a few surfers in the water, dancing along the waves. It's getting late, and the sun is setting, so it's only the pros that are out there now.

I like to drive by the beach to have a think sometimes. It clears my head. I like to feel the salt wind on my face and the soft sand under my feet. It makes me feel alive and present in the moment. I'm not the biggest fan of mumbo jumbo meditation or things like that, but I do like to sit on a near-empty beach and enjoy the last rays of sunlight for the day.

This afternoon with Skipper had been simply magical. My heart skips a beat when I think of him now. The phenomenal sex we had in my classroom, just like the old days. I'm going to remember that for a very long time; if not in my head, then at least in my body. Skipper can do things to me that I've never felt before. He knows exactly where and when to push me, to play me like a fiddle. I love it.

But I do worry about him. About who he is. Yeah, I might've lost myself in his intense lovemaking, but now, sitting on the beach, my mind clears, and I'm reminded about who he is and what he did to me. The pain he caused me. Sure, he's apologized, but is that enough? Should I let him off the hook just because he said a couple of pretty words? Can I really forgive and forget? When I look at his face, will I always be reminded of that moment when I opened the door to the bedroom at that house party eight years ago and saw him on that bed with my best friend? Will I ever erase that moment from my mind?

How do other people do this?

I take in a deep breath, taking in the fresh ocean air.

No. It'll take *actions*, not words, to satisfy me. I'll have to see what Skipper does before I can pass judgment on him. He can't just say some pretty words, he actually has to *live* by them.

Then maybe my heart can truly forgive him.

I sigh and run my hands through the soft, warm sand. It's nice out here. Nice to be alone with my thoughts, however raging they are.

A figure runs out from the waves and jogs towards me. A surfer. He's waving in my direction and I raise a hand to block out the setting sun in order to see him better.

It's Cove, my brother.

"Hey, sis!" Cove sprints up to me sitting on the beach, a long surfboard under his arm. He's dripping wet. My brother is tall, probably the same height as Skipper, and slightly skinnier. He's very athletic after all the training he's been doing for his surfing competitions. I still can't believe my brother is a pro surfer. A few years ago, he was partying hard in clubs and screwing girls left right and center. Now he's happily married to my best friend and living the life, traveling the world and doing major competitions.

"Hey, Cove."

"I thought I was seeing you sitting on the beach. I had to come over to check."

"Yeah, it's me."

"What are you doing here?"

"Not much."

"How're things?"

Cove shrugs. "Everything's great. Ripley's doing pretty good at her job. She's happy at the hospital, but you probably know that already."

"I didn't."

My best friend and I haven't spoken much in the last few weeks.

"Really? She was saying how you two should catch up soon. I think she'll really like that."

"Yeah, we haven't had the chance to lately," I reply. "It's mostly my fault. My life's been a crazy mess."

"A mess? You mean work or your love life?"

I laugh. "Both."

"Fucking hell, Sandy. Drama. You're worse than me."

I smile weakly. "I guess it runs in the family."

"Do you want to talk about it?" he asks, sitting down beside me on the sand, placing his surfboard to rest at his feet. He brushes sand off his hands.

"It's complicated, but you remember Skipper Deep, right?"

"Of course, I remember Skipper. He was at our wedding; I think Dad invited him or something."

I sighed. "Yeah, of course Dad invited him. Skipper's a billionaire who basically owns his family's massive company in America, so of course Dad would've loved him to be at your wedding."

"Typical Dad. And I remember this Skipper guy from, like, a decade ago when you two used to date. Wait, he's the guy who fucked you over, if I remember right, yeah?"

"Yeah, he did," I reply. "He's back and we've kinda... begun things again."

"No fucking way, sis." Cove laughs at me. I roll my eyes at his mocking attitude. My little brother likes to tease, especially when the problem is not about him for once. "You're crazy, Sandy."

"As I said, it runs in the family."

"What are you going to do? Date him?"

I pick up a handful and sand and watch it fall through my fingers. "I dunno. My head's a mess."

"You like this guy?"

"Yeah," I say, nodding. It's like I'm nodding to myself, like I'm telling myself I know I really do *like* Skipper, despite our past. I really do like him. "I just hope I'm not another fling to him."

"You're talking to the wrong guy here," Cove says with a chuckle. "I used to be a playboy, so I can't give you any advice. I'm not the right man for this."

"How did you know with Ripley? When did you know you were in love with her? How did you know you were going to stop your playboy lifestyle?"

Maybe he is the right man to ask. If anyone could get Ripley, then they must be doing something right.

Cove sighs. "It's cliché, but you just *know*. Just see how he acts around you. Even the best actor in the world can't hide their feelings when they're truly in love with someone. I dunno."

"Right."

"You know me, though. I'm just a horny idiot. What do I know?"

"You snagged Ripley, that's something."

Cove smiles and looks out at the horizon. "Yeah, that really was something. Lucky me." He's being genuine. Really genuine. It's rare to see my brother like this – this much *in love* - but Ripley's brought it out of him. She's like a witch with magical powers, doing the impossible. Making my little brother a normal person.

"But I just don't know about Skipper. I don't know what he's thinking. I don't know if he won't screw me over again."

Cove stands, picking up his surfboard with a grunt. "This really sounds like something you should talk to Ripley about," he says. "Call her. Really, I mean it. She'll want to talk to you about this."

"Yeah," I reply. "I think I will."

"I've got to go. I've got an early flight tomorrow."

"A surfing competition?"

"Yeah."

"Whereabouts?"

"Hawaii."

"That's amazing."

It really is.

I'm proud of him.

Cove waves at me and starts to jog up to the parking lot, his surfboard flapping under his arm. "It is! See ya, sis."

I smile at him as he disappears, and I turn back to watch the ocean. The sun is nearly gone below the horizon.

Maybe, with Skipper, my heart is opening up.

Maybe I have already forgiven him.

Maybe I should open myself up to the possibility of love.

21

SANDY

Iᴛ's deadly quiet inside the long room. The only sound is of pens scribbling on papers.

Wait.

There is a sound, I hear it.

Whispering. Some chatting among students.

"No talking," I say, my raised voice echoing around the silent room. The students, all sitting at separate desks, seem to freeze, frightened of my sudden voice. The air in the room is full of tension and stress. My students think they're feeling it, but little do they know how much more terrified and stressed I am than they.

It's the English exam. The big day. The day I've been dreading for months.

This exam is important. *Super* important. My students' average marks from this English exam will be compared with the average marks of all the other subjects. It's the way the school judges what subjects the students are doing well in, and what subjects they're doing badly in. It's what the school uses to judge the teachers.

What they're going to use to judge me.

And you don't want your kids to do badly in this exam, and you *never* want to be the teacher of the worst-performing subject. Especially when you're me and it's clear that my job is on the chopping block here.

That's what Mr. Brown and Miss Tweed said.

I scan the room. Each student has their own individual desk, separate from each other and all facing me. I can see them all from the comfort of my chair. I can see if there's any cheating or any talking. It's what I'm supposed to do, but inside I'm freaking out because I don't want any of them to fail.

They've all been amazing the last few weeks, studying Romeo and Juliet hard. I've drilled into them all the aspects of the plot and story, all in preparation for this exam. I hope they're okay. I check around the room for any cases of students stressing. I can't help them with the answers, but I can give them some encouraging words. I used to freak out massively over exams when I was their age, so I know what it's like. I don't want any of them to go through what I did.

My eyes rest on Tom and James. The two trouble-makers have come a long way in a month or so. Skipper's been amazing with them, teaching them in his own wacky style. They love him. The boys look up to him, and who wouldn't? Skipper's funny, relaxed, witty, smart, and has made a lot of money in his life. Any teenage boy would look up to him.

And so do I. I love watching Skipper tutor. He's a natural. If he didn't go into being a billionaire international businessman, then he would've definitely have made an excellent small-town teacher.

Tom and James pour over their exam papers, their heads

bowed. Neither of them has looked up so far since I started the clock. That could either be a good sign or a terrible one. I'll just have to wait and see.

My pocket buzzes. My phone. I pull it out and check it. Skipper's name pops up and I decide to read his message.

How's the exam going?

I type back quickly. And quietly.

Don't know yet, could be really good or really bad.

Skipper replies straight away.

You're an amazing teacher. I'm sure everything is fine.

I close my eyes upon reading that message. When he decides to be nice, he's great. Skipper's been on his best behavior for the last few weeks, ever since that kiss on the beach. I think he's really after me. This thing we're doing isn't just a fling. He really wants me. He's been making all the good moves.

I mean, he's been *amazing* in bed. We've met up a couple of times, usually sneaky flings after school in one of the locked dark classrooms. It feels so naughty to steal some time in the empty school; it's like we're horny teenagers again. Skipper always knows how to pleasure me in all the right places. He's so attentive and simply... *there*. I do feel special with him. I'm not just another girl. I do see the desire in his eyes when he looks at me. He calls my name out when he climaxes.

But what happens when he decides to go? He can't stay in New Water forever. He's going to decide whether or not to invest in Poseidon's Academy, and either way, he'll leave. And I don't want to leave here; this is my home. What happens if he decides not to invest in the school? What then? I've been too scared to raise the subject with him, too scared of the answer. What if he decides not to commit to me at all like he hasn't yet with the school?

What if he drops me like he did eight years ago?

I sigh and return my phone to my pocket.

Then the bell rings. The end of the exam.

"Okay," I announce to the class. "That's it. Put your pens down. I'll come around and collect your papers."

I stand up and immediately get to work, picking up the answer sheets from each table. I won't be marking these papers. It's got to be an independent process, so they're getting posted to an independent adjudicator to be judged. I just hope my students have done well.

I come across James and Tom. They're sitting at a desk apart.

"How do you think you went, boys?" I ask, picking up their answer sheets.

They both shrug and mumble at me. Typical teenage boys; communicating through monkey grunts. I take it they don't even know how they went in the exam. This just sets my heart rate faster.

Oh, no.

With all the answer sheets taken, the students leave. All filing out the door and back into the school grounds. As they leave, a shadowy figure appears at the doorway, letting them pass.

Miss Tweed.

She's here? What for?

She waits until all the students have left the room, smiling at each of them with her frightening smile, and then steps into the room. I'm busy clearing up and putting the exam tables and chairs back into place. I try to ignore her, but she shuffles up right up to me, still smiling.

"Did the exam go well, Miss Finn?" she asks in her high-pitched voice. I pick up a nearby chair and place it neatly against the wall, trying to show her my nonchalance at her presence. But Miss Tweed doesn't care. She's here to insult me, I know, and she isn't going to stop.

"I think so. You never know with these things, don't you? Even the students don't know."

"Well," Miss Tweed replies, following me around the room. I can't deal with her stalking me like this. "Hopefully English is not going to be the worst subject in these exams, for your sake."

"For my sake?"

"I've still got my eye on you, Miss Finn. Don't you forget that."

I've had enough of this.

I turn around then, dropping the chair in my hands. I'm facing the small woman now. Her puffy hair reaches my nose. "What do you want, Miss Tweed? What do you want?"

Miss Tweed blinks as if taken aback. She gasps in fake surprise.

Oh, she's mocking me.

"I want you to get fired, Sandy," she says without hesitation. "I want you to get sacked. I thought you knew that."

I really can't believe this. I can't believe how blunt she is. Miss Tweed wants me sacked and is unafraid to admit it. She's just simply *horrible*.

"You've really got it in for me, don't you?" I ask, crossing my arms.

"Your firing is so close to happening," she says. It's like she's enjoying every minute of this, like she's savoring the venomous words that drip out of her mouth. "Oh, and don't forget the school fundraiser at my house on Sunday night. I really do hope you can make it, Miss Finn."

She smiles at me one last time, then waddles out of the room back through the door. She's gone.

What a bitch.

Great. I'm worried about the exam, worried about Skipper, and now worried about Miss Tweed working day and night to fire me.

What fun times.

22

SANDY

THE ELEVATOR DOORS ping open and I step into the hotel hallway, turning my head left and right to spot the signs as to where I'm going. But I don't need to find out what direction I need to go.

This particular hotel room practically covers the entire top floor of New Water's luxury hotel.

This whole floor is dedicated to one room.

The Presidential Suite. Also known as the hotel room Skipper Deep is staying in.

I walk down the hallway from the elevator, and I see his bodyguard standing outside the door. He gives me a silent nod as I approach, recognizing me.

"Hi, Steve," I greet.

"Hello, Miss Finn."

"Is Skipper home?"

"He is," Steve replies as he turns to knock on the door, but I quickly raise my hand over his, stopping him.

"I'd prefer to knock," I say, smiling at the bodyguard.

Steve nods back and lets me pass. I've met him a few times in the last few weeks. I guess Skipper's that big of a deal - or at least he thinks he is - to warrant a twenty-four-seven bodyguard.

I take in a deep breath and tap my fist on the hotel door.

It takes a moment for Skipper to open up. He doesn't expect me here tonight. He thinks I'm decompressing after the exam earlier today, but I want to surprise him. I've never actually been to his hotel room, or more accurately, suite, before. And I've come especially dressed tonight. I've got a sexy black dress on. And no panties.

Oh, I'm really gonna give him a big shock.

The door swings open and there he is. The tall man. My heart still flutters when I see him.

And he's standing there in his underpants, clearly assuming to be answering the door to only his bodyguard.

He clearly doesn't expect to see me standing at his door with a skinny black dress on.

Clearly, I'm the last person he expects to open the door to.

"Jesus, Sandy, you scared me," he says, eyes wide.

"Good. It's time you felt something," I reply. I step into his hotel room without waiting for him to invite me in. I keep strolling in until I'm standing in the middle of the living room and until I get a full view of the presidential suite. I sway my tight ass in my black skirt with every step to give Skipper something to look at as he closes the door. I deliberately don't pay him any attention as I saunter in. I like to tease.

Wow, the presidential suite is massive. And what a view. You can see all of New Water laid out below in one big panoramic view from the presidential suite's window. The horizon stretches on below until you can see the white beaches and the blue water. The sun is just dipping below the horizon, bathing the town in a beautiful red glare.

The room itself is decadent. Everything looks so expensive. I've been in some fancy places in my time as a daughter of a billionaire, but this is one of the best hotel suites I've ever been in. I can see the marble bathroom from here. The baby grand piano sitting invitingly in the living room. The massive TV screens. The private kitchen fit for a mansion. Everything is here to really scream out you're a billionaire.

And Skipper Deep definitely is one. And proud of it.

Of course, he's staying in this room. A place fit for a king, that's what Skipper sees himself as.

But right now, he's looking a bit embarrassed. He didn't expect to see me. He didn't expect to open the door to me in just his underpants.

He's flustered.

And I like it.

"Wait there while I change," he mutters, face red.

"Aw, I like what you're wearing," I reply as he scrambles towards the bedroom. "Keep it on."

"Help yourself to a drink," he shouts as he ducks into the master bedroom. I smile and follow him inside. He's trying to put on a suit when I stroll up to him and place a finger on his lips.

"Don't bother getting changed. You'll only be getting out of it in a moment," I say, leaning forward to kiss him tenderly on the mouth. He kisses back. His hands reach around my back to help take off my dress, but *no.*

Not this time.

"This time I'm in control," I whisper between kisses.

I remove his hands from around my body and instead push him down on the king-sized hotel bed. He falls onto his back and I climb on top of him, straddling him between my legs. I smile and bite my lip as Skipper looks up at me.

"Holy shit, Sandy," he says, but I raise my finger back up to his gorgeous lips.

"I've had enough of you talking, bad boy," I command with my best sexy teacher's voice. "How about you be silent and let me punish you for being so naughty?"

"Yes, Miss Finn."

A moment ago, he was just in his underpants and now this sexy woman's dominating him in his room.

I feel his warm body below me as I work my hands over his goddamn perfect abs. They're rock solid. He shouldn't be real. A shiver runs down my hands as my fingers brush his muscular pecs. I lean over and begin to kiss his open mouth again, thinking of his lovely jawline as I start to pull down his underpants. I feel his giant cock spring out against my leg. Oh, he's already erect.

Well, I'm already wet.

"Time for your detention, naughty boy," I moan as I position myself over his bulging erection and push him inside me. My wet pussy welcomes his cock eagerly, lapping him up.

Skipper groans as he enters me, but I hush him again, pushing my finger into his mouth. He sucks.

And I begin to ride him.

I rock my hips as Skipper thrusts into me.

I know what he likes, and he knows what I like. The moves he did to make me gasp and moan. I involuntarily run my hands through my hair and bite down hard on my lip as he does things to my body I can't explain. Skipper works me hard. He knows how deep to go to bring me to orgasmic joy. His smile as he does so turns me on even more, his perfect, confident smile as he playfully fucks me to oblivion. Heat pulsated through my body, getting stronger with every thrust of his engorged member into my soft, wet pussy.

I'm pushed to the brink and I feel my legs stiffen around his. I come again and again in waves of pleasure.

"Fuck me," I moan as I'm completely spent. I remove myself off his cock and scoop down, pulling his member into my warm mouth. He can't hold on for long, as mere seconds later he comes between my lips. I accept his hot load greedily. Skipper groans and calls out my name as he comes.

I fall forward and wrap my arms around his muscular body.

We're both completely spent, just like we've sucked each other dry of energy.

I snuggle into him and close my eyes as he hooks his thick arm around me.

23

SANDY

SKIPPER'S HAND gently grazes my shoulder as he curls into me from behind on the bed. I push back into him, my warm ass digging into his groin. My mouth hangs open and a rush of air passes through it as Skipper moves in closer to hold me tighter in this hot embrace. I am literally gasping for him like an eager animal. This position we're cuddling in is perfect.

This is the place for me.

Skipper slants his head forward from behind and tenderly whispers into my ear. The silk bed sheets swoosh as he moves. His hot breath tickles my skin, tingling me all over. "How about I order some champagne?" he asks.

I moan softly in the affirmative and delicately push my body even further against his. My round ass fits snugly around his exposed cock.

Yes, champagne would be great right now.

I rub my ass against his member and feel it start to get hard.

From behind me, Skipper's spare arm reaches to his bedside table for the hotel telephone. It clicks when he picks up the receiver.

"Hello, yes. I would like a bottle of your finest champagne, please. Two glasses." He hangs up and his free arm now finds its way to my buttocks. He squeezes my ass cheeks with his muscular hand, and I yelp sensually in response. "You like that, kitten?"

"Mm," I moan. "I do, big boy."

He really knows how to turn me on, doesn't he?

I am *aching* for him, for his cock. I want him to fill me up.

But, as if to tease me, Skipper lets go of our embrace and pulls away from me. I pout in sexual frustration as he lifts up his side of the silk bedsheets and steps out of the bed. In annoyance, I slowly roll over to his side of the bed, pushing myself into the hot comfy crevice left in the mattress by his body. I hazily open my eyes to watch Skipper casually cross the master bedroom and head to his waiting clothes.

He bends over to pick up a new pair of underpants and I admire his toned ass. His body is lightly tanned all over and it's clear from where I'm lying that he never ever skips leg day. His legs are muscular and brawny, just the way I like my men. Skipper is a fine specimen of a man in his physical, and may I say *sexual*, prime. He's like a tough, strong bear. I feel safe lying in his bed, like he can protect me from anything.

"Where are you going?" I ask him with no real urgency. I wish he'd come back to bed, come back and please me as he did earlier. I would like that very, *very* much.

"I don't want to greet room service completely naked," Skipper replies, finding a spare shirt in his deep wardrobe to put on.

"Why not? I think that's kind of hot."

"I've already greeted someone today in just my underpants, and look how that's turned out," Skipper replies, gesturing to me lying in his bed. "I can't keep filling up my bed with people who've come to my door and find me irresistible wearing just my underwear."

"True that. Just stay naked for me, okay?"

I lie here, in his massive bed, as he continues dressing, not knowing what's going on in his mind. I want to know. I want to see what Skipper Deep is thinking in that gorgeous head of his, but I don't know at all. I have no clue. It irritates me. I want to understand him. I want to know our future.

I want to know if he truly likes me as he says he does, or if this is just another time where he'll run off to a different girl again.

"What do you think about the school?" I dare to ask.

"Poseidon's Academy?"

"No, the other one I work at," I reply sarcastically.

"Shut up, you."

"Do you think you're going to invest in it?"

Skipper ponders my question for a moment, then shrugs his shoulders and bends down to slide his trousers over his gorgeous legs. "I'm still to make up my mind," he replies. "I don't know yet."

I really wish I could pry open his head and see what he is thinking. Will he invest in the school? Will he stay in New Water? What happens if he decides to go back to America?

What will happen to me?

"When do you think you'll decide?" I ask, lifting my head up on the pillow so I can see him better. I don't like pushing him like this, but I need an answer.

I can't bear not knowing.

"When the time's right."

"When do you think it'll be right?"

Skipper chuckles as if I'm being a silly girl and strolls back over to me on the bed. He still needs to button up his shirt; his solid abs are showing. He kisses me for a brief moment and runs his hand through my post-sex crazy hair. "Don't worry about it," he whispers.

But I am worrying. I kiss him back. His face is cool to the touch. His lips are full and inviting. I just want to stay in bed with him for a whole week and never leave. I just want to make love over and over again. Just us two. That's the dream.

As our tongues meet, all I can think of are Miss Tweed's words to me. Her threat. Those venomous words echo in my head.

I've got my eye on you.

She really does. She's really out to get me fired from the school. She wants me gone. I've never had someone hate me like her, someone who actually passionately despises me.

And I can't trust Skipper. He says not to worry, yet I can't help but worry. What happens to me when he decides to go? Will I be left all alone like I was eight years ago? Will he abandon me again? Find some other woman to keep his hotel bed warm?

Sandy, you've got yourself in a tricky situation. You're falling for a man you can't trust.

Skipper stands again and starts to button up his shirt.

Bye, nice shiny abs.

I continue watching him and his beautiful body, thinking of what to prod him with next. I need to calm the raging questions and doubts in my head.

"Did you hear about Miss Tweed's fundraiser?" I ask him.

"No, not yet."

"It's at her house on Sunday night. I hate these things. How about you come along? I need you to be there for emotional support. I can't do these things alone."

Skipper smirks. "Ask me nicely."

"Please."

"Ask me again."

"Mister Skipper Deep, please can you come to Miss Tweed's stupid fundraiser?"

Skipper strokes his chin. "It's at her house?"

"Yes."

"Okay, I'll come."

I smile at him and he smiles back.

I really don't have a single clue as to what he's thinking.

DING.

The doorbell to the presidential suite rings. Skipper winks at me and dashes out of the room to answer it, only to reappear a moment later with a wine bucket and two glasses. He brings the bottle of chilled champagne sitting in ice to the bedside table.

I sit up properly against the silk pillow, covering my breasts with the bedsheet, and observe Skipper popping open the bottle. He does so with a satisfying relish. *POP.*

The lovely sound of bubbles fills the air as he pours us both a glass, bringing mine over to me in bed.

We cheer, chinking our glasses, and I taste the refreshing champagne. Expensive stuff.

"Here's to the future," Skipper says before he sips on the golden liquid.

"To the future."

I smile, but I'm still left wondering. Wondering if this may be the highlight of my time with Skipper.

Maybe this might be the best time, and everything is downhill from here.

What will happen to me? What will happen to us?
Will he abandon me like he did eight years ago?
Am I enough for this billionaire businessman?
Is there even going to be a future for Skipper and me?

24

SANDY

THE EARLY MORNING light temporarily blinds me as I unlock my car door and step out into the beach parking lot.

"Hello, Sandy." The voice surprises me, but I would recognize that American accent anywhere.

Ripley Sailor, now Ripley Finn. My best friend and sister-in-law has her car parked right next to mine. I didn't even see her when I drove into my usual space.

"Hi, Ripley," I greet. She's arrived before me and she's already unpacking her surfboard from her car. Closing my driver's door, I run over to her side and give her a big hug. She laughs as I squeeze her tight. We've arranged by phone call to meet here in order to surf together before the beach gets too busy.

It is high time I see my best friend. We haven't spoken for weeks.

"Nice and early," she says, and I nod in agreement as I put my hand up over my eyes to protect them from the rays of morning sunshine shining down on us and the beach.

"It's the best time to come," I say. "It's really good to see you. How are things?"

"All good! Work at the hospital's been great and Cove is doing well in Hawaii. I think he's going to win this tournament. He says he saw you here the other day."

"Yeah, he did." I turn to collect my own surfboard from my car.

"He says you seemed a bit down. Restless."

I shrug. "I wasn't, really. I've just been thinking a lot about things, you know?"

"Hm. That doesn't sound good."

"No," I reply. "It's nothing like that. There's just a lot going on in my life at the moment, that's all."

Yeah, Skipper and Miss Tweed and potentially losing my job. Those little, minor things.

"You want to talk about it?"

I shake my head slowly. "Maybe not now."

"You okay?" Ripley asks in her soft accent.

"I'm fine. Just a lot happening."

My best friend laughs. "It's strange that you're the one who's going through something. Usually the drama's happening with me."

"I guess."

"You've been a good friend to me, Sandy."

"You too."

"You can always talk to me. You've always been there for me, but remember I'm here for you."

I nod. I still don't want to talk about Skipper and my job and all that, but it's good to know Ripley's got my back. That she's still my best friend. That we're still a team. "Got it."

"Come on," Ripley says. "Let's catch the waves before everyone arrives."

I can't agree more.

We rush down to the surf and start paddling out into the ocean. There's only us and the crazy old surfer dudes out in the waves this early, but it's going to be a nice day and we anticipate the beach will fill up soon with families and tourists. Once we paddle far out enough, we sit on our boards and enjoy the sunrise together, waiting for the next good wave to come.

"You've become really good at surfing," I say to my best friend. Ripley snorts and waves me away.

"Cove has me out here all the time now. You just have to get good when he's with you, like it's the law or something."

"Ripley, you're talking to his sister; I know that exactly. He's the only reason I can surf. I picked it up out of nowhere just being around him. It's like learning by osmosis."

"So, tell me what's really going on," Ripley asks, changing the subject. "Why are you *thinking* so much at the moment? Why did even Cove, the tone-deaf idiot he is, notice you seeming a bit down?"

I take in a long breath.

Might as well tell her.

It's been dominating my thoughts for weeks. It'll be good for me to get it off my chest.

"I'm kind of seeing Skipper Deep again."

Ripley's jaw falls open at the mention of his name. I've told her ages ago about him and what had happened between us.

"Skipper Deep? What, as in that guy who cheated on you, like, a decade ago? *That* Skipper Deep?"

"Yeah. Him," I reply. "He was at your wedding. That's where we met again."

"To be honest, there were a lot of people at my wedding that even I didn't know."

"Yeah, Dad likes to invite his friends. He treats everything like a business meeting, including his son's wedding, it seems."

"So, you're saying that you re-met Skipper Deep at the wedding and have rekindled some kind of fling with him?"

"Well, that's the problem," I whisper.

Ripley shakes her head in disbelief. "Oh, no. Don't tell me you're *falling* for him again."

I wince. "Kind of."

"*Sandy.*"

"I know, I know," I reply. "I'm an idiot, I get it. But he's really the only man for me. It's like my heart's been waiting for him all these years and hasn't let go. It's like he completes me. God, that sounds so stupid, saying it out loud. You know what I mean."

"So, you basically love him. What's the problem, then?"

"He lives in America."

"Oh."

"And he's only here for a short time, for business reasons. He's thinking of investing in Poseidon's Academy."

"Wait, your school?"

"Yeah, but I just can't get the future out of my head and what this all means. What happens when he goes back to America? Has all this between us just been a fling for him? Is he going to leave me, or worse, cheat on me again?"

Great. All my words have just come out in one big rush.

"Damn, girl. I thought I had problems with Cove."

I sigh. "I wouldn't be able to cope if he cheated on me again. He promises he'll never do it, that the first time he was drunk and a stupid teenage boy, but I just can't fully trust his words. I'm afraid to commit and then have my heart broken another time, just like it did eight years ago. I can't go through that pain again, Ripley. I just can't."

She slowly nods. "I understand completely, Sandy. It's a

hard place to be in. Cove was like that for me. I couldn't trust him at first."

"So, what made you?"

"It was his actions, not his words. Cove proved his love for me through what he did and how he acted, not with empty promises or nice talking points."

Exactly what I want to do with Skipper.

Actions, not words.

"So, I should judge him on what he does and not what he says?" This is already obvious to me, but hearing it from the mouth of my best friend makes everything make sense. I need to hear this from somebody else for it to seem right.

"If he really loves you, Sandy, he'll fight for you. He won't even need to say anything. He'll prove it with what he does for you. Trust me, you'll know. I knew with Cove. Boys can say anything, men do *things* to prove their love."

I smile at her and she smiles back. She's right. I know she's right. I can't listen to Skipper's promises, no matter how sincere I feel like they are. No matter how much I want to trust him. I have to see him show his love by what he does. If he truly loves me, then I'll be able to see it. I'll know when I do.

"It's good to see you, Ripley," I say.

"It's good to see you, too."

The next series of waves approach. I steady myself and bite my lip in anticipation. I want to enjoy this morning of surfing with my best friend. I will.

"Let's catch this wave," I say. And we do. Together.

25

SANDY

I GET the message from him just before I set off.

Hey, Sandy. I'm getting there early. No rush.

I grab my car keys from the ceramic bowl I keep them in by the front door and head out to the car, replying on my phone as I skip outside.

No problem. See you soon x

So, Skipper's there at Miss Tweed's house, nice and early. What fun that'll be for him, just them two together.

Now, that's a party I'm sure he'll enjoy.

I get into my car and turn on the ignition. I reverse out of my driveway and onto the street, following my phone's GPS to Miss Tweed's house.

The fundraiser. What a great way to spend my Sunday night. Well, at least Skipper's going to be there to make it slightly less painful. Seeing him will get me through the next few hours of agony.

I can picture the scene at her house already, plates of cheese and crackers with cheap wine and Miss Tweed's strong perfume clogging up the air. I've never been to her house and I plan to never again, but I can really imagine what it smells like even before I arrive.

Just get through tonight. Stick to Skipper. You'll be fine.

When I told her, in passing, that Skipper was going to make an appearance, Miss Tweed seemed to not be able to contain herself with the news. I reckon she's in love with him. Great. Another weird thing to do with Miss Tweed; she wants to fire me *and* steal the man I'm with.

How can she get worse?

It takes a while to get to her house as she lives on the other side of town. My phone guides me around the narrow suburban roads until I'm at her front door. A normal-looking house. I park out on the street and sit in the car for a moment, composing myself. Readying myself to go inside.

You'll be fine. Stay with Skipper. Let him take care of you.

I need to be ready to face Miss Tweed. I check my makeup in the car mirror like it's an armor I've put on to protect myself from the teacher. I'm all good. I look good.

"You're sexy, Sandy," I say to myself. "You've got this."

I take in a deep breath and exit the car. The sun is setting. It's getting dark. It's time to go in and face Miss Tweed.

Just get this night over with.

At least Skipper will be there to hold my hand and guide me through.

I step up to her front door and ring the bell. Miss Tweed opens the door. Her fake smile immediately disappears once she sees me.

So, it begins.

"Oh, hello, Miss Finn. I'm glad you're here. Do come inside," she says, standing aside to let me through. Her house is like an extension of her school office. Photos of sunsets and old family members line the walls. The place smells of her cheap perfume, just as I predicted. It's all a bit... tacky.

Just get this over with. In and out.

I follow Miss Tweed through the front hallway and into the living room.

There are a few people here already. Mingling around. Some familiar faces. I smile at a parent I know.

Where is he? Where's Skipper?

And, just as I expect, there's cheese and crackers set up on the table. They appear hard and inedible. Ten points to me for guessing correctly. Miss Tweed is so predictable.

She appears at my side. "Mr. Brown isn't here yet," she whispers sternly at me. "You better get to work talking to people. Do the one thing you can do and get that money, Miss Finn. Your job is on the line."

As if I didn't know that.

She doesn't have to keep reminding me of it. I've been *very* aware of how close I am to losing my job the last few days.

The things I imagine doing to her are unspeakable.

"Where's Skipper?" I ask her, ignoring her command to start networking immediately.

Miss Tweed likes my question. She really puts on her big fake smile this time. "Oh, he arrived early. I think he went upstairs to have a private conversation with Becky."

What?

I nearly spit out my dinner in shock.

"Becky? Becky Taylor?"

Miss Tweed bobbles her little head, which shakes her massive puffy hair. "Yes, she's a lovely girl that Becky. They looked like they were deep in conversation," Miss Tweed says, leaning towards me. "If you ask me, they looked like they were flirting. They're both very attractive people, so I can see the connection."

My vision narrows and my heart rate speeds up. This can't be happening.

Becky Taylor? The bitchy single mom who's out to sleep with every guy she can get her hands on? She's here, and she's talking to Skipper? Flirting?

And they're both upstairs?

Fuck.

In a panic, I quickly make my leave and rush out of the living room, heading up the stairs. I reach the next floor of Miss Tweed's house and make my way through the hallway.

No, this can't be happening.

It's like a nightmare.

It's just like how it was eight years ago.

It can't be happening. This should be a dream. This shouldn't be real.

I open up the first door. It's the bathroom. I immediately turn and continue down the hallway. I open another door, bursting through this one marked *Office*, and that's when I see them.

Skipper.

And Becky Taylor.

Skipper is sitting down at Miss Tweed's desk and Becky is sitting on his lap, facing him.

And her tits are out.

Her tits are exposed and are in his face. Her *naked* giant tits.

In Skipper's face.

I don't do anything. My mouth drops open and I am stuck to the spot.

This is a nightmare. This is a nightmare. This is a nightmare.

But I don't wake up.

This is reality.

Hearing the intrusion into the office, both Skipper and Becky turn to face me. Becky's mouth transforms into a big grin when she recognizes me.

"Please knock," she says to me across the room with her smirk widening even more. "We're busy."

I ignore her and focus my attention on Skipper. He looks disheveled, shocked at me entering.

"*Skipper*," it's all I can manage to blurb out before I turn around and walk straight out of the room and back into the hallway. I don't even bother to slam the door behind me.

I am in total shock. I can't even feel my body as I hold on to the wall for support. I can't even breathe.

This truly is a nightmare.

This can't be happening.

It's just like it was eight years ago. The same circumstances. The same feeling.

One sentence runs through my head over and over.

Skipper's cheated on me. Skipper's cheated on me. Skipper's cheated on me.

It's too much for me to bear. The pain is too real. I want to collapse. My knees buckle and I sink to the floor. Tears rush to my eyes and I want to moan in pain, but no sound comes out of my mouth.

Skipper's cheated on me. Skipper's cheated on me. Skipper's cheated on me.

Someone's behind me. They're lifting me back to my feet. I know that touch anywhere. The strength. The muscular hands.

Skipper.

"Get your hands off me," I growl, shaking my arms away from Skipper's hold. I fall against the wall, wishing to wake up.

But this is really not a dream.

"Sandy," he softly whispers. "Sandy."

But I don't let him talk. I don't let him speak. I don't need to hear his words, his lying pretty words. I've seen what he's done in that room. He can't take back what he was up to.

Eight years ago. Repeated.

"You lying coward," I say, my mouth so wet with anger I'm spitting. I can barely get the words out. "You told me. You *promised* me. Why did I ever trust you? I'm such a stupid idiot. A fool."

"Sandy, let me talk."

"You have nothing to say. You're nothing but a liar. You've used me. You've taken advantage of me and I welcomed you back. I should've thrown you out like garbage. You came back into my life with your *smile* and your pretty face and gorgeous body and you thought you could just use me. And you did."

"Please, Sandy," Skipper mutters. "Let me explain."

"Fuck you, Skipper. I'm not listening to you anymore. You betrayed me."

And that's enough.

I need to get out of here.

I storm away from him, away from his grasp. I stagger down the hallway and down the stairs. I rush past Miss Tweed, who's standing on the stairs, clearly listening in, and out the front door into my car.

26

SANDY

ONE HAND CLUTCHES the steering wheel, and the other hand is clasped tightly around the shifter. My knuckles are white with tension. I'm driving, but I don't know where. I'm just driving and driving. Down and around the bendy streets of New Water. I've got no plan as to where I'm going. I just need to keep moving. I need to stay focused on something, and not let my mind wander back to that house, back to that office, back to what Skipper was doing with or to Becky Taylor. I can't let myself think about that.

Keep going, Sandy. Keep moving. Don't stop. Don't let your thoughts consume you.

I keep driving away from Miss Tweed's house, my mind completely blank. Purely focusing on the next turning or the lines on the road lit up by my car's headlights. It's dark now. Night. I just want to get as far away as I can from Miss Tweed's house.

And that's how I end up at the beach. I don't know why my subconscious drove me here, but once I arrive at the beach parking lot, I feel like it's the right place to be. It's the right place for my mind. I park in my usual space. The entire parking lot is deserted. And I get out of the car.

I can't believe it. I was an idiot. Why did I trust him?

I stagger, in the dark, down to the sand, and I sit facing the shadowy ocean. The sand is still warm. It's nice to just sit here. It's only me and the crashing waves and the dim moon high in the sky.

I sit back and close my eyes.

Peace.

Quiet.

I'm alone.

But inside I'm fuming. Burning. Raging.

I always knew Skipper would do this. Why didn't I trust my instincts? I always knew he would cheat on me again. I should've listened to my gut. Why did I think I was so special that he'd change his whole life plans for me and stay in New Water? Why did I have the inflated ego to think he'd stick to his pretty little promises?

Why would I think he would be any different from who he was eight years ago?

He saw me at Cove and Ripley's wedding and thought I was ripe for the picking, that even after all these years, I'd fall for him again in less than a heartbeat. And he was right. He just used me for his own closure. It must be really nice in his head right now, thinking that even though he fucked me over once, he had the good looks and the charm to do it all over again.

Yeah, Skipper, you're a handsome bastard. You can do this to anyone you like. You've proven that tonight.

Anyone will fall for him, and he has the power to snap his fingers and ruin their life. He knows that now. He did it to me.

Actions, not words.

I fell for his words.

But tonight, I saw his actions.

I should've listened to Ripley. Instead, I just fell back into being that silly little teenage girl again, fawning over the hot man in the nice suit.

I've been so stupid. So awfully stupid.

And now my heart is paying the price for my stupidity.

I pull my phone out. The bright screen on the dark beach blinds me for a moment, but my eyes quickly adjust, especially when I see the notifications.

Ten missed calls.

All from Skipper.

I've only been gone from Miss Tweed's house for less than half an hour and he's been trying to call me and message me multiple times. I don't care what he has to say. I don't want to listen to his nice little lies anymore. I'm not going to be persuaded again by his endless charm. This time, it really is over. No more nice Sandy Finn.

I think about what I want to say for a second and then I type out a message to him.

Don't bother investing in the school. I never want to work with you. I trusted you and you fucked me over. I never, ever want to see you again. Got that? Never. You should grab your bags right now and fuck off out of New Water, just like you did eight years ago. Bye forever.

And that's it. I press the icon. Sent.

And then I block his number from my contacts. I really never want to hear from him again. Then I put away my phone.

I sigh, and tears start forming in my eye. Floods of tears. I'm breaking down.

I'm sitting on this empty beach at night and I'm crying my heart out. There's no one around. No one to see me like this. I just feel so alone. So empty. So cold.

In one night, my world has shattered.

Just like it did back then at the house party when I was a naïve teenager.

What excuse do I have now?

Of course, Skipper Deep cheated on me. It was my fault for trusting him again. It's the exact same thing that happened eight years ago. I trusted that man with his perfect smile and solid abs, and I got burned for it.

I never learned.

I told myself for years that I was over him, that I'd matured. That I was a strong, independent woman who didn't need a man to satisfy her. Not me.

But then Skipper Deep sauntered back into town and I, being such a weak fantasist, believed his lies only to be torn up again.

I let him do this to me.

I didn't listen to my better judgment. I screwed up.

And I've now sent him an emotional message.

And now I don't want to hear what he's got to say. I don't want to hear his pitiful excuses. This time, I'm not going to give in to his cocky attitude. I never want to see him again.

My phone buzzes in my pocket. It can't be Skipper; I've only just blocked him. I check who it is.

Mr. Brown. He's messaging me at such a late time? On a Sunday?

My heart stops. This must be serious.

Hello, Miss Finn. I will be needing to speak to you first thing in the morning before classes start. See me in my office as soon as you get to school.

I throw the phone down on the sand beside me.

Not this as well.

My heart really does stop now.

I've been knocked out here like a bad boxer twice in one night. A double whammy.

This message from the principal can mean only one thing.

My job is over. I'm getting fired. That's it.

Bye, bye teaching career.

That means, on the same night, I've lost the love of my life and my job.

Great.

Taking the top spot off that house party eight years ago, I think I can safely say that this is the worse night of my life.

27

THREE HOURS EARLIER

SKIPPER

I ARRIVE at Miss Tweed's house early on purpose. I park my car across the road from her place and stare out the window. The sun is going to set soon. Before I get out of my vehicle, I type out a message to Sandy on my phone and send it to her.

Hey, Sandy. I'm getting there early. No rush.

I hope she actually follows what my message asks and doesn't rush to get here. There's a lot for me to do before she arrives.

I can't have her around whilst I do what I have to do.

I open my car door, step up to Miss Tweed's house, and ring her bell.

DING DONG.

It's like she's been waiting for me. She opens the door

almost immediately after I ring. Seeing me standing at her doorway, the mathematics teacher gives me the biggest smile.

"Well, hello, Mr. Deep. Fancy you arriving so early."

"Yeah, I guess I am."

She gestures at me excitedly, ushering me inside. "Come in, come in, make yourself at home. You're not the first to arrive."

I follow her through the hallway and into her living room. Her place reminds me of her office. I'm not trying to judge, but her interior designing is very, very tacky. Not my style at all, but that's just me.

There's another guest here in the living room. I recognize her. It's that Becky woman from the previous fundraiser, that one I couldn't get to stop trying to flirt with me. The one with the fake tits and the fake face. She's the only other person here, and she's already on the wine. She clutches a glass like it's as precious as a baby. This Becky woman flutters her eyelashes at me as I enter and immediately floats across the center of the living room towards me before I can duck away.

"Hello, Mr. Deep," she coos as she reaches my side. Miss Tweed hangs by my other arm. Great, I'm alone and surrounded by two women who both seem ready to carry me off to bed right now.

How can I get out of this one?

"Ah, hello, ladies," I mutter. Miss Tweed offers me a glass of wine, but I gently refuse. I'm not here to drink or to fraternize with the dolled-up single mothers of the school. I'm here to work.

I need to get this done before Sandy arrives.

Becky struts even closer to me and rests her hand on my shoulder. Her big tits graze my sleeve. "You're looking *fine* tonight, Mr. Deep," she says. "I like your suit. It looks very expensive, and I like expensive things."

Her fingers play with my suit collar, her long manicured fingernails slightly scratching my neck. It's like she's got her claws around me.

What have I done to get into this position?

I take a step back. "Miss Tweed," I say. "Where's the bathroom?"

"It's upstairs, darling. First door."

"Thanks."

I need to make my exit. As I head to the stairs, I hear the doorbell ring. More guests. Good.

I head up to the next floor. I'm not really searching for the bathroom; I'm looking for her office. And when I see the door marked *Office,* I murmur softly to myself.

"Bingo."

I've found it.

Checking over my shoulder for anyone following me up the stairs, I quickly open the office door and slide into the room, turning the light on as I quietly shut the door behind me. This place looks like it's got what I need. Books line the shelves and there's a row of filing cabinets stuffed full of documents. The room is a bit messy, just like her office at school, but I can work with that. All I need to do is find the financial records.

I sit down at her big desk and rifle through the papers scattered around. Nothing is interesting to me. I bend over and start opening the drawers. I find some information related to the school's tax reports. Perfect. I flick out my phone and take a photo of each page. I lean further down and open the bottom drawer.

And that's when the office door opens.

I glance up. I've been found out. Anyone who stumbles in will immediately know I'm up to something shady.

It's Becky. She's standing in the doorway with a glass of wine in her hand. She's tipsy, but she's glaring at me. She knows I'm up to no good.

Fuck.

I do look guilty.

"Hello, Mr. Deep," she says, her voice slurred from the alcohol. "What are you doing in here?"

She must've followed me up the stairs.

I curse myself for not being more thorough, checking no one was behind me.

"I'm just snooping around," I reply. It's better to be more honest about it and pretend that I'm just curious so that I can hide the fact I'm actually taking photos of Miss Tweed's financial records of the school. Nothing wrong with a little white lie. "I just want to see what Miss Tweed's house looks like."

"Well, other guests have started arriving, so Miss Tweed is busy downstairs. No one will bother us up here." Becky slowly closes the door, keeping her eyes on me the entire time as she crosses the room.

Oh, damn.

I realize what she wants.

She wants to fuck me.

I can't be dealing with this right now.

I hide my phone back into my suit pocket just in time as Becky saunters around the desk.

"I'm about to head back downstairs," I say.

"No, you won't," she replies, placing her glass of wine on the desk. I make a move to stand, but Becky kicks forward with her high heel, pushing me on the chest back down to the chair. "Not if you don't want me to tell Miss Tweed you're up to something naughty in here."

She licks her filled lips and places her hands on her dress, right at her cleavage.

This is not good. I need to get out of here. I can't be dealing with a drunk Becky trying to clumsily seduce me in Miss Tweed's office. It was a mistake trying to sneak in here for the tax documents. I shouldn't have come here tonight, but when Sandy said the other day that the fundraiser was at Miss Tweed's house, I couldn't resist. I knew tonight would be my one big chance to snoop around to find her financial records. But I shouldn't have come, and now look at the predicament I'm in.

I can't get out.

Becky has me trapped here.

"Do you like what you see?" Becky asks as she slowly pulls her tits out of her dress. She shakes her ass, doing a little drunk dance that she thinks is sexual. I'm just stuck to the chair, thinking of an excuse to get out. I don't want her ratting on me to Miss Tweed. I don't want the teacher finding out I've been snooping around in her home office.

Becky's fake tits have popped out of her dress and she waves them in front of me.

Fucking great.

Then she comes forward and sits down on my lap, facing me. She waves her giant tits in my face. All I want to do is get out of here.

And then the door slams open.

Both Becky and I turn our faces to the intruder.

It's Sandy.

No.

I'm in shock.

Sandy glares back at us. I see the surprise, terror, and shame in her eyes.

I see her heart break right in front of me.

I see it shatter.

And it's all my fault.

No.

All I want to do is tell her that this isn't what this looks like. It looks bad, but I did not consent to this. I didn't consent to Becky drunkenly throwing herself at me with her naked breasts in my face.

I'm not in the wrong here, no matter how bad this looks.

But I know Sandy won't be seeing that, or even what's really going on right now. She's instead seeing what happened eight years ago at that cursed house party. She's seeing me as that past version of me, that stupid teenage boy who screwed her over just like this. And to be honest, I don't blame her for it.

She has every right to think that.

I know this looks terrible, but it's not what it seems.

Sandy leaves the room and I force Becky off me.

"You're going to pay for this," I whisper in her ear as I gently push her aside and rush out of the office. She mumbles something drunkenly after me, but I don't care what she says.

Sandy's collapsed on the floor in the hallway and I help her to her feet, but she throws accusation after accusation at me even as I try to explain myself. But my words are useless. They fall on deaf ears. Sandy won't listen to me.

And, after what my past self did to her, I really don't blame her.

Fuck past me. One mistake has ruined me forever.

Sandy storms off, down the stairs, and out in the street into her car. I don't follow her. I know she needs a moment to decompress and to breathe without me trying vainly to make excuses. I head back down the stairs, ignoring Becky swaying, drunk, behind me.

Miss Tweed's leaning on the banister, clearly listening in. She reaches out and holds my arm as I pass, stopping me in my tracks.

"Oh, I do apologize for young Miss Finn's behavior,"

Miss Tweed says. "And I also apologize for her behavior over the last few weeks whilst you've been here. I'm sorry you've had to endure her. Don't worry, though, I'm going to make sure she gets fired as soon as possible. We can't have her tarnishing the reputation of Poseidon's Academy."

I lean in towards the teacher and whisper. "I want to let you know that I've decided not to invest in the school now. Tell that to Mr. Brown."

Without waiting for Miss Tweed's response, I am out of there. Out of her house. I jump into my car and speed off.

In the car, I try calling Sandy multiple times on loud-speaker. She doesn't pick up, just as I expect. I speed back to my hotel.

This is all my fault. Sandy's right to jump to the conclusion that I was cheating on her with that Becky. She has every right to feel like that when I fucked her over so badly all those years ago.

But it isn't true.

I didn't want Becky's tits in my face.

I didn't want to be trapped there in Miss Tweed's office.

I head straight up to the presidential suite and I place my phone on the table, waiting for her response. I know Sandy. I know her so well. I know she will either call me or message me. I sit down and wait by the phone. Waiting. Waiting. Waiting.

In a few minutes, my phone lights up with her message.

Don't bother investing in the school. I never want to work with you. I trusted you and you fucked me over. I never, ever want to see you again. Got that? Never. You should grab your bags right now and fuck off out of New Water, just like you did eight years ago. Bye forever.

Immediately I try calling her, but my number can't reach through.

She's blocked me.

Damn.

I have to explain to her what happened. I have to prove to her that I'm not the cheating, lying man she thinks I am.

I need to make this right, and I need to do it fast.

28

SANDY

I GET the email exactly when I step into the school, like as soon as I step through the front gate into the grounds from the staff parking lot, there's a ping announcing an email notification.

What is it?

My phone's deep in my bag somewhere. I pull it out and check the email. I have to read it twice to fully comprehend what it's saying. It takes a moment for the contents of the email to sink in, but when it does, I'm gob smacked.

The exam results.

They're in from the independent adjudicator. The email's saying they've marked all subjects and have averaged all the scores already. *Wow,* they've been quick.

I can't see the individual results of any particular student, but I scroll through until I find English.

No, it can't be.

But it's written there in black and white. Clear as day.

My eyes scan over the text once, then twice, then three times before it sinks it properly.

No way.

My class has received the highest average mark out of all the subjects, including mathematics. Miss Tweed's subject. I'm the teacher with the highest average marks of all the classes, beating everyone. Even beating Miss Tweed.

No freaking way.

This is incredible. My teaching has pulled through. Romeo and Juliet has pulled through.

I lean against the doorway of the school and scroll through the email, just double checking that I'm reading this right. And I am. I have the highest average scores of any subject, even more than Miss Tweed. That must be a first.

But then I realize something.

It's too late.

It no longer matters what marks my students got from my teaching. There's a reason I'm at the school this early in the morning.

The meeting with Mr. Brown.

That's why I'm here.

I'm going to get fired, email or no email. Good scores or not.

I couldn't sleep at all last night after what happened at Miss Tweed's house. I stayed, reflecting, at the beach until it was early morning, then I went home and sat in bed awake until it was time to shower and come here. It was a stupid move, but I knew that I wouldn't be able to sleep even if I tried. The night's events plagued me like a waking nightmare I couldn't escape from. I realize I haven't shut my eye once in the past twenty-four hours. My mind has endlessly been replaying the scene at Miss Tweed's house over and over in my head like a film. Repeating it until it's seared into my vision. An echo in my head telling me over and over how much of an idiot I'd been trusting Skipper Deep again.

Him, sitting at that desk, with Becky's big fake boobs rubbing into his face. They were moments away from his cock entering her.

How could I have let this happen to me?

I was so deeply and utterly embarrassed last night. I don't think I can ever recover from it.

Skipper has emotionally scarred me for life. Twice.

And now I'm at school about to get fired, no matter what the results of the exam are.

The worst night of my life is turning into the worst day as well.

I compose myself in the school hallway and head on down to Mr. Brown's office, knocking on the door. It's time to face my executioner.

Take it as a strong woman. After last night, it's all I've got left, my small remaining amount of dignity and self-respect.

"Come in."

I do.

Mr. Brown is sitting at his desk, and next to him, standing, is Miss Tweed. Just as she was in my last meeting in here. But I don't expect to see her in here now. My eyes dart over to her and she looks back at me with a snarl.

Oh, boy.

Of course, she's here. There'll be nothing she loves more than twisting the dagger into her helpless prey. I'm a rabbit caught in a trap. No escape. Here's my fate.

And I bet she's going to enjoy it.

"Please sit," Mr. Brown says, motioning at the chair opposite his desk. I do. "There's no easy way to put this, Miss Finn."

"Easy way to put what?" I'm not going down easy, not after that email I've just seen.

Mr. Brown sighs. "Miss Finn, it's been a tough decision to make, but I'm sorry, you're getting let go by the school."

I knew it.

"I'm getting fired?"

"Well, you can put it like that."

"For what?" I ask. "Did you just get the email about the exam results? Did you read what it says? The kids got a better average score in English above all other classes, including math."

I'm not going down without a fight.

Mr. Brown goes silent. He's not great at confrontations, or when he knows the person he's talking to is correct.

And I've one hundred percent correct now.

"Sweetie," Miss Tweed interrupts, leaning across the table and flashing me her fake smile. "The average scores of the students aren't the reason we're firing you. No. We're firing you because you've lost the school Skipper Deep and his money. He's told me personally that he's not going to invest, and so, therefore, you're being let go, that's why. It's your fault he's not investing. Your fault. And you have to pay."

"Pay with my job?"

"I'm afraid so, Miss Finn."

Look at her face. She's so fucking happy.

"Why do you think I'm the reason he's not investing? Do you have proof of this?"

Miss Tweed shakes her head. "Oh, we know everything about your little... liaisons with Mr. Deep. I overheard you last night at my house. Your little argument was very illuminating."

"You don't know anything."

"I think I do, young miss."

She throws something down on the desk. Papers. I lean over to get a closer look at them. *No*, not papers. They're photographs. Pictures taken of Skipper and me. One of us kissing together at the beach, another one of me holding the towel in front of his naked body, another one of me entering his hotel. All taken on a long lens like paparazzi photos in a trashy tabloid.

"What are these?"

"They're photographs, can't you see?"

"Photos of Skipper and I?"

"Exactly, Miss Finn," she replies. "They're evidence. Proof of how you've purposely sabotaged the school."

Oh.

Now I know what's happened; she's paid a photographer to stalk me for the last few weeks and take photos of me and Skipper from a distance. And now she has those photographs spread out over Mr. Brown's desk. Photos of my personal life. Photos of Skipper and me. Miss Tweed turns her head to look at me and tuts. "I did tell you, *Miss Finn*, that I've got my eye on you. And now, if you try to apply for a teaching job at any school in the country, Mr. Brown and I will pick up that phone and tell them everything about you. Everything. We'll say you're a slut and a liar, purely out to wring money from the school, and who can't be trusted."

Holy cow.

The woman's insane. And a stalker. And clearly obsessed with Skipper. And obsessed about hurting me in every way.

But this crazy woman has control over the school through her stranglehold on Mr. Brown, and she's getting me fired. She's kicking me out of my dream job at my dream school. The same school I went to as a kid. She's going to ruin my professional reputation forever. And, judging from

Mr. Brown's blank expression, there's absolutely nothing I can do about it. No amount of protesting can save me now.

I'm doomed.

I'm at a loss for words. Miss Tweed smugly smiles at me like she's won some kind of competition between us. But I never wanted a competition with her or anybody else. I *just wanted to teach.*

And now that's over.

"Can you see now why we have no reason but to fire you," Miss Tweed says.

"Can I be excused for a moment?" I ask, my throat dry. My hands shake.

Mr. Brown waves at the door, letting me go for a minute. Miss Tweed just looks on in pure, unfiltered joy as I stand up and walk out of the office, closing the door behind me.

I'm alone in the deserted hallways of the school. I cover my face in my hands and, for the hundredth time today, I begin to cry.

My entire world, everything, has collapsed around me. Skipper's revealed to me exactly who he is. My job is lost. Everything I love or care about is burning around me.

I just stand there in the hallway of the school I love and sob. I don't care if Mr. Brown and Miss Tweed can hear me from inside the office behind me. I don't care about anything anymore. I'm a loser. A failure.

BOOM.

The double doors at the end of the hallway burst open with a slam. I flick my head up to see what's going on. Someone's entered the hallway.

The school doors have opened, and it's Skipper Deep that is walking through. Coming towards me.

29

SKIPPER

As I SWING OPEN the hallway doors, I see Sandy Finn crying there outside the principal's office.

The first words out of her mouth are venom.

"What the fuck are you doing here?" she shouts at me, her voice echoing down the hallway. I ignore her and continue marching towards her and the office. Steve, my bodyguard, stays close beside me. "I said, Skipper Deep, what are you doing here?"

We ignore her words.

I reach her, stopping a few yards away from her, close enough to see the tears streaming down her face. I can clearly see from the redness of her cheeks and the tears in her eyes that she's angry, hurt, and confused.

Just as I thought she would be.

A dangerous cocktail of emotions. I need to tread carefully here.

"I've come back to talk," I say.

She glares at me, and I see her tears have quickly

changed from ones of sadness to ones of anger. "The time for talking is long gone, Skipper. You can't say anything to me that'll change what you did last night. I don't want to hear anything from you. I don't care what kind of *talking* you want to do."

"No, listen..."

"No, you listen, Skipper. Can you, for once, imagine the pain you've caused someone else? Do you have any empathy in you at all? My heart's been hurting since you fucked my best friend all those years ago. And now you've torn it out of me again. *Again*. Do you know how much of an idiot that makes me feel?"

"I wouldn't know," I reply. "But please, just listen to me..."

"No, you wouldn't know. You're always so perfect with your charm, and your smile, and your beautiful body. I bet you've never felt like an idiot in your life. And that's why I'm not going to listen to a single damn word that comes out of your stupid mouth."

That stings.

She's wrong. I have felt like an idiot before, like a big idiot. The day I cheated on her. When I thought I'd lost her forever. That's when I've felt like an idiot, like the biggest idiot on the planet.

"Sandy, I'm not here to talk to you," I say calmly. I don't want to inflame this any further.

"Then why are you back?"

"I'm not here to talk to you. I'm here to talk to the principle of Poseidon's Academy."

Sandy blinks, mouth agape, as she soaks in this new information. She doesn't expect me to say this, that I want to talk to Mr. Brown. "What?"

"I know I can't explain what happened last night with just my words, so you'll have to see for yourself."

"What are you talking about? I saw what you did last night. I saw what you were up to with Becky with my own two eyes. I saw your face between her tits."

"Let me show you otherwise."

"Show me what? Nothing you can say will change what I saw."

"I would like you to come into Mr. Brown's office with me and listen to what I've got to say," I reply softly.

"No."

"Please."

"I said *no*."

"Hear me out on this, Sandy. Trust me."

"I can't trust you," she says. "Not anymore."

"I know, but just come into the office and at least see for yourself."

"Go back in there? I can't."

"Please, just see what I'm here for."

Sandy shakes her head sadly.

"I've been fired, Skipper."

No.

I hang my head. "I thought you would be. That's a shame."

"Just a shame? They're firing me because you're not investing in the school. They're blaming the entire financial ruin of the school all on me, so thanks for that. Thanks for ruining my life. And Miss Tweed even has photographs of us two together."

"Does she now?" I raise my eyebrows. I didn't expect that. Very sly of the older teacher.

"Yes, she does."

"Okay," I say. "Well, how about you come in and see what I've got to say?"

30

SANDY

Skipper doesn't even wait for me to reply before he knocks on the door to Mr. Brown's office.

How about you come in and see what I've got to say?

That's what he's asked me to do, so I'm going to do it, just to see what kind of excuses flow from his mouth. I'm not going to trust a word he says, but if he's ready to lie to everyone, then so be it. I'm going to watch him and catch him in the act.

What he's got to say? What does he mean by that? And why is he here?

I want to reply to the man that I don't care what he has to say, but I'm actually curious why he's come here.

He says he's not here for me, but to talk to Mr. Brown. Why?

Skipper seems calm. Composed. Even after my screaming match at him, he's not bothered. He hasn't raised his voice against mine or seemed perturbed by my raging emotion. It's not what I thought would happen when I saw him enter the school hallway a moment ago. It's like he knows something I don't. An ace up his sleeve. Either that or the cocky man is unfazed by anything.

He might just be such an arrogant dick he doesn't even give a shit about my feelings.

I follow him inside the principal's office.

As soon as she notices Skipper entering the room, Miss Tweed straightens up like she's standing to attention. Her cheeks flush.

She's obsessed with him.

It's embarrassing to see.

And my own face isn't much better. I try to wipe away the tears with the back of my hand, but I know it's useless. My face is red and stinging from crying too much. I must look like a blubbering mess.

Great, I'm exposing myself to Mr. Brown and Miss Tweed in my moment of weakness.

Mr. Brown sits up in his chair, obviously not expecting Skipper Deep to be walking into his office early on a Monday morning with his bodyguard. He's the last person Mr. Brown is expecting to see.

But Skipper ignores all of us and calmly strolls into the office with Steve and me following.

The whole atmosphere of the office has changed now that Skipper's entered.

"What a surprise, Mr. Deep," Mr. Brown says, gesturing to the spare chair, but Skipper does not sit. He continues to stand by the door. I'm stuck behind him like he's a shield between me and Miss Tweed, but I prefer it this way. I don't want to be the center of attention. I want to be as small as possible. "What can I do for you, Mr. Deep?"

"I've come here today to let you know I'm reconsidering my stance on investing in the school," Skipper says, and Miss Tweed and Mr. Brown's expressions both change into smiles. They're immediately happy about this sudden change in the school's financial situation.

"That's very good news, Mr. Deep," Mr. Brown replies, but Skipper gently raises a hand to silence the principal.

"I've concluded my orientation here. Unfortunately, it's turned into a bit more like an investigation."

Mr. Brown is very clearly confused about this sudden change. "An investigation? About what?"

"Someone's been stealing from the school, Mr. Brown."

The room goes silent. Mr. Brown shakes his head.

"That can't be the case."

"Oh, unfortunately, it is."

"Who's been stealing? Why? How?"

"You wouldn't know about this, Mr. Brown, but I've had my private team of lawyers and accountants hard at work the last few weeks reviewing the financial situation of the school. I've had them pouring over the school's tax documents," Skipper replies. He remains perfectly emotionless and calm as he delivers the information. He's completely professional. It's strange seeing him like this, in full-on work mode. But it's also kinda sexy. I would be fancying him right now if it wasn't for what he did last night.

"A private team of lawyers and accountants? I don't understand."

"What they've discovered is that, for the past five years, someone's been stealing from the school."

"Stealing?"

"Yes, and I know who it is."

"Who?"

"The information is quite... sensitive."

Mr. Brown's face reddens. "Well, please tell me, and let's get this over with."

"You want me to say it out loud, here?"

"Yes, sir."

"Well, it took us some time to discover who the culprit is, but it's you, Miss Tweed." Every head in the room, including Skipper's bodyguard, turns to the mathematics teacher.

Her?

Miss Tweed?

Is what Skipper's saying true?

She's been stealing from the school?

I mean, she is the bookkeeper of the place, but I would never think she's been stealing. And for five years? That sounds crazy.

We all turn to her and immediately her face drops.

Miss Tweed looks guilty as hell.

It's obvious she does not expect this accusation right now. She frantically flips her attention between the principal and Skipper over and over, her face getting redder. She lets out a nervous squeak of a laugh, trying to dismiss it.

"What?" she stutters. "Me?"

"Yes, you."

"No, that's impossible. Little old me?"

"Oh, it's you, Miss Tweed," Skipper coolly continues. "You're the person stealing from the school."

"That's not right."

"Seeing that you've been doing it for five years and you're the sole bookkeeper of the place, you've stolen quite a lot. You've been lying to Mr. Brown here and you've been skimming off a lot of the tax for yourself. No wonder the school's in dire straits."

"This is simply not true."

Skipper ignores her. "Poseidon's Academy doesn't have a problem with raising money, but it's losing a lot due to you, Miss Tweed."

I watch this all unfold with shock disbelief. Skipper is on the attack here against Miss Tweed, and she's quivering in fear. This is what he wanted me to come in here for, or is there more to be unraveled?

I'm so confused.

"Where's the proof, Mr. Deep? You can't just accuse me of anything unless you can prove it."

Miss Tweed thinks she has Skipper caught now with her logic. Her surprised expression reverts back to her smug smile.

For a moment there I was deluded to think Skipper had won, that he'd one-upped Miss Tweed, but she's still a wolf amongst sheep. She knows how to play this game.

She's a fighter, and she's going to fight back.

I hope Skipper is right in his accusation because otherwise there'll be hell to pay.

"You did say you wanted to work with me to cut the riff-raff out of the school, Miss Tweed. Now I've found out it's actually you who's the riff-raff."

"You need *evidence*, Mr. Deep," she replies. "You need proof before you can sling these kinds of words in here in front of me."

"Don't worry about proof, Miss Tweed. I've got a whole load of evidence. Documents and documents of tax receipts and files that my team has gathered. There's a whole lot of paperwork I have ready. My team of accountants and lawyers have all the numbers, and they all point to you."

Miss Tweed's face drops.

He's got her.

It's very satisfying.

I didn't think I'll be seeing this all happening when I came in expecting to be fired this morning.

"I don't understand what I'm hearing," Mr. Brown mutters, and, for once, I agree with him. I don't know what's happening. But Skipper clearly does. He's so restrained and serene, like he knows exactly what he's doing. He has this all planned out.

"I am angry," Skipper says. "Not about the school's money. I don't care about that. I don't even care about one stupid teacher skimming off tens of thousands a year. What I care about is the person I love the most in the world getting heartbroken. That's what has really got me angry, and I think you know what I'm talking about, Miss Tweed."

The person he loves the most in the world? Their heart broken?

Is he talking about me?

Miss Tweed's giant puffy hair wobbles as she shakes in apprehension. "I don't know what you're talking about, Mr. Deep," she stammers.

"Oh, I think you do. Tell Sandy here about how you tried to frame me."

What?

"I never did."

"Don't you lie. Not on this."

"I've never tried to frame you. I don't know what you're talking about."

Skipper takes in a deep breath, and his composure slightly cracks. I see through this calm façade he's putting on. There's something boiling underneath. He's full of anger. Miss Tweed spots it too and immediately shuts up.

Skipper Deep is furious.

"Okay," he says, restraining his emotion with a toneless delivery. "Fine then."

He nods at his bodyguard. Steve leaves the office only to return a moment later, pulling in the arm of someone.

Becky Taylor.

The bodyguard has brought in Becky Taylor. The woman I last saw flashing her tits into Skipper's face.

What's going on?

Why is she here?

Her face is also red, and her cheeks are wet. I realize she's also been crying. She glances at me, horrified at the sight of me. Me being here scares her somehow. I don't know what Skipper's said to her, but she's upset and terrified.

Skipper turns to her, disgust in his eyes.

"Tell them what you told me, Becky," he says in a threatening voice.

She blubbers and lets out an indecipherable whimper.

"Tell them what you told me," Skipper repeats, eyes on the parent. She's frightened of him.

Becky sobs. "Miss Tweed bribed me with better marks for my son if I'd, in her own words, 'ambushed' Mr. Deep upstairs at the party. I didn't want to do it, but I was drunk, and she said my son would pass Math if I did it."

The room is stunned by this revelation. Mr. Brown slowly shakes his head, not believing what's happening.

And I don't believe it too.

It was all a lie? A set up by Miss Tweed?

Becky had cornered Skipper?

Had I got everything wrong last night?

Was I blind to the truth?

This is all happening too fast for me to digest.

Miss Tweed is freaking out. Her puff of brown hair really starts to wobble as she twists her head from person to person. She's realizing she's losing her grip on power by the second. Skipper is out to get her.

She's scared. Miss Tweed is actually *scared*.

I've never seen this before.

"I did that for the good of the school," she tries to explain to Mr. Brown. "Sandy is a terrible teacher who deserves to be..."

"SHUT UP."

The room falls silent.

Skipper has shouted. He's lost his calm composure. He's screamed at Miss Tweed and everyone looks at him, petrified. Stunned.

The tall, muscular billionaire holds all the power in the room.

He's a real man.

My man.

Skipper exhales and then speaks very quietly, clearly trying to hold back his anger. "You have been trying to get me to invest in this school, Miss Tweed, and therefore, you've tried to steal my own money. But, worse of all, you're trying to insult the love of my life. You're calling her a terrible teacher? I can never let that slide. I have been working with Sandy for the last few weeks coaching her troublemaking students and, let me say on the record, that I think she's a wonderful teacher. You, though, Miss Tweed, are not a teacher. You are a criminal." Skipper turns to Mr. Brown. "Maybe now's the time to get the police involved, sir. Miss Tweed's stolen a lot of money and I have the photocopied documents to prove it. I'll send the evidence to you via email once I leave. Then I suggest you call the police. I'm sure you don't need my help to find their number."

And that's it. Skipper turns around and heads out of the office.

But before he does, he spins back around. "Oh, yeah, I almost forgot. I'm not going to invest in the school," he says to the principal. "I'm actually going to buy it. And my first act as owner is to have Sandy reinstated. Does that sound fair?"

He waits for Mr. Brown to answer. The principal doesn't speak for a few moments, digesting what's been said.

"Uh, yes. That's fair."

"Good."

Skipper leaves the office. I follow him out the door, hearing Miss Tweed break down in tears after me. She's blubbering out pitiful excuses to Mr. Brown, who's completely ignoring her.

In the empty school hallway, Skipper turns to me, acknowledging me for the first time since he stepped foot inside the principal's office.

He gives me a wink. "So, Sandy, did you listen to every single damn word that came out of my stupid mouth, then?"

31

SANDY

"I don't know what to say."

Skipper smiles at me as I stutter out the words and it's like a thousand fireworks explode in my chest all at once. I'm still processing what just happened in that office, but I know it was good.

I know that everything's changed.

Skipper just came into the school, and Mr. Brown's office, like a whirlwind, changing the whole scenery. One moment I was hating him, the next I'm practically thanking him.

He's a force of nature.

But there's still so much to think about.

A million things rush through my mind in the school hallway as my man smiles at me. Skipper's company is buying Poseidon's Academy? Miss Tweed's been stealing money? I'm to be reinstated? It's all too much.

Too much to take in.

I honestly don't know what to say.

"You don't have to say anything," he replies.

"But, last night, in that room... I thought that you..."

"I know," Skipper says, reaching out and wrapping his arms around me in a strong embrace. "I would never cheat on you, Sandy. I've made that mistake once already and I've paid for it every day since then."

"I can't believe this."

He was set up.

I'd seen the wrong thing.

I was lied to.

"You're the love of my life, Sandy. I would never hurt you again."

"Yeah?"

"All of this," he says. "All of this was for you. I haven't been able to get you out of my head for eight years. Eight long years. I've needed you every minute, Sandy, since I left you all those years ago. I made a big mistake back then, and I've come back to rectify it. I came back to New Water for you."

"You did?"

"I need you, Sandy. My life is incomplete without you. I'm begging you to forgive me for what I did. You're the love of my life, and I promise you I will never hurt you again."

"I forgive you, Skipper. I do."

And then I let go and I melt into his arms. He really does love me. I refused to see that he did, I was too scared that he was going to cheat on me again that I made up a whole other narrative in my mind. It was like I was *waiting* for him to cheat again when I should've been watching what he was actually doing. Everything he was doing was for me. The financial records of the school. Miss Tweed. Him being here. This was all for me. I should never have doubted his love. Skipper places a finger under my chin and lifts my face so that we're staring into each other's eyes.

"I'm so sorry," he says. "For everything. I love you, Sandy."

Those are the words my heart's been aching for eight long years to hear, and I know they're true. Skipper has shown his love for me in so many ways.

He really does love me.

I was blind to it, but now I see.

"I love you too."

RING.

The school bell goes, echoing loudly down the hallways. The doors slam open and students start to swarm inside the school around us. I keep my eyes on Skipper, and he keeps his eyes on me until I'm suddenly tugged away by someone below me.

Skipper and I break our embrace as I'm pulled away from him. I look down to see who it is.

James has run over and hugged me. His little hands reach around my waist as he buries himself into my jeans.

"James! You're hugging me?"

Tom's suddenly here as well. He runs up and joins James in his hug around my legs.

What the hell? These two troublemakers are actually *hugging* me. My heart's fit to burst by their abrupt cuteness.

"What's happened, boys? Why are you hugging me?"

"I passed my English exam," James shouts. Tom joins him too.

They both passed English.

Skipper bends his knees down to their level. "How about that, guys? What do you say to Miss Finn for helping you?"

"Thank you."

"Thanks, Miss Finn."

I shake my head and mouth *I love you* to Skipper.

He grins back at me.

"Maybe I'll have to just get you guys some video game vouchers," I say jokingly to the boys, and Skipper laughs.

We did this together. Skipper and me. We taught James and Tom all about Shakespeare and now they've passed the important exam. A few weeks ago, they couldn't be in the same room together without fighting, and now they're best friends. Kind of like Skipper and me.

A few weeks ago, they didn't even listen to one word I said in class, and now they're passing Shakespeare.

Thanks to Skipper.

Thanks to me.

Skipper leans over the two boys and hands me a note. I don't have time to look at it before he's walking away. Out of the school.

Wait.

I move to chase him down, but the two boys have me tightly locked in their hug.

They're very cute, but they're not helping me at all.

Before I know it, Skipper disappears out the school doors. Gone.

And I can't follow.

Damn.

"Thanks, guys," I say to the two boys. "But maybe that's been a long enough hug."

They giggle and run off together, pretending to shoot each other.

I unravel the note Skipper passed me. It's a detention slip. I roll my eyes.

Cocky bastard.

I read what he's written on it. There's only a sentence.

Meet me after class.

And then there's the name of his hotel.

Alright, Skipper Deep. You win this time, you cheeky man.

32

SANDY

As THE ELEVATOR ascends the many floors of the luxury hotel, I play with my hair in the elevator mirror, making sure it's just right.

My hands shake as I run them through my hair. I'm nervous. I don't know why I am; I'm only meeting Skipper, just like he asked me to do on that detention note. I shouldn't be nervous about anything right now, but I am.

The events of the day pass by me in a blur. That whole confrontation in the principal's office still replays through my mind. I can't get Skipper's words out of my head.

He loves me.

And I love him.

So, he wasn't cheating on me last night at Miss Tweed's house, instead he was set up by that malicious teacher. She wanted me to break down and break up with Skipper. She wanted him to leave New Water because of our argument, so that she had an excuse to fire me. She had photographs of us together. She wanted me gone, and she very nearly succeeded if it wasn't for Skipper riding in to save the day at the last moment. I should never have doubted him for a minute.

So, for the last few weeks, he's been gathering evidence of Miss Tweed's stealing? With his crack team of lawyers and accountants? He never told me anything about that.

I judged Skipper too soon. He has been trying to do the right thing. He's proven he really loves me, and I've been too blind to see what kind of man he truly is. I was so blinded by what had happened eight years ago.

I've spent the whole day back in my classroom. I was immediately reinstated by Mr. Brown after Skipper's revelations. I was even spied Miss Tweed being led to a police vehicle through my classroom windows. It was hard not to notice her; she was spitting and yelling and resisting the cops every step of the way, her puffy hair shaking about like ruined candy floss.

I knew it was bad to enjoy the spectacle of her being arrested, but I did enjoy it very, *very* much.

The elevator doors ping open and I step into the hotel hallway leading to the presidential suite. Steve, the bodyguard, stands to attention.

"Hi," I say.

"He's waiting for you," Steve winks at me.

I hesitate before knocking on the hotel door leading into the suite. Sweat builds on my forehead. I am super nervous.

I knock.

And Skipper opens up and I gasp when I see him. For once he's not wearing an expensive tailored suit, but instead a wetsuit and, under his arm, he's carrying a surfboard. He looks like a pro surfer. The sight of him dressed that way, surrounded by the luxury confines of the presidential suite, makes me giggle.

"Hey, don't laugh," Skipper says. "I thought we'd go out for a surf together."

Instead of replying, I reach forward and pull him close to me, going for a long kiss. Our lips meet and he kisses back.

So, he wants to go for a surf?

Then I'd better get ready.

* * *

WE SIT on our boards in the middle of the ocean. It's a busy time of the day to come surfing. We're surrounded by others paddling out on their boards as well. We're all waiting for the next set of waves to come.

I skim my hand across the surface of the bobbling ocean, feeling the cold water.

Thinking about the day's events.

Skipper and I have recounted them all, him explaining why he did what he did. I've asked him a billion questions, but one thing's for sure.

He loves me.

"You never told me about your investigation into Miss Tweed and her stealing the money. Why?" I ask Skipper as he leans back on his board next to me.

"I couldn't," Skipper replies. "I didn't want a conflict of interest. I needed to keep it secret whilst we completed our investigation, even from you."

"Even from me?"

"I'm sorry to cover it up."

"You could've trusted me."

"We had to keep it secret."

"Don't worry. You did the right thing," I reply. "You caught her in the act, and that's what matters."

"I'm glad it worked out."

I smile. "Me too."

"Her face though when I revealed the dirt I had on her, wasn't that great? I loved that moment."

"Yeah, it was priceless."

"I'm glad you got to witness that, after everything she did to you."

I pause. I want to ask him the question, the question that's had me nervous all day. The question that's been on my mind. I need to know his answer. "Skipper, so what happens with you now? Are you going to head back home to America?"

Skipper pauses as well. His eyes flicker, scanning over the horizon. He turns to me and speaks. "I think I'm gonna stay here, if that's okay with you, Miss Finn."

Yes.

He leans over and kisses me. I fall into his lips. His reassurance. He tastes of saltwater and a hopeful future.

Skipper Finn is staying in New Water.

It's everything I've ever wanted. This morning I went into school thinking that my love had cheated on me and I was going to get fired from my dream job. I thought it was going to be the worst day of my life, and yet now I'm ending the day knowing my job is secure, surfing with my love, and knowing he's going to stay with me forever.

Skipper breaks our kiss. "I need to stay. I need to make sure this school my company's just bought heads back on track after years of mismanagement. And then we'll probably expand into Australia, buy more schools, so I'll be needed for that."

"That's the only reason you're staying?"

"Oh, no, it isn't. Most of all, the love of my life is here, and I'm never going to leave her again."

I wink at him. "Well, you have been a naughty boy. Maybe you do need some private tutoring."

"Oh, I'm sure you can arrange that, Miss Finn."
He doesn't need to tell me. I already am.

EPILOGUE

THREE MONTHS LATER

SANDY

"You LOOK SEXY," Skipper tells me.

I know I do.

I spin around and check myself out in the mirror. I'm wearing a new blue dress, something Skipper bought for me. It fits snugly on my body. I check it out in the reflection, tracing my eyes down my side. The dress curves around my round ass.

Yeah, I do look sexy.

We're actually in my classroom at Poseidon's Academy, but today is not just any other day, hence my gorgeous dress.

Today's the reopening of the school.

Skipper's company did buy out the entire school and today's the big day where they'll throw a big party and reopen the place. After five years of mismanagement and Miss Tweed stealing the money, it's time for Poseidon's Academy to relive its glory days, and I can't be more excited. I know this party's going to be a million times better than all the awful school fundraisers Miss Tweed used to throw. This is Skipper Deep's party, and the man knows how to have a good time.

And for the last three months, Skipper has kept true to his word, staying in New Water to oversee the business arrangements of buying, and then reopening, the school. I've been with him every day through this whole process. He moved out of the hotel's presidential suite, and into my house, and, more importantly, *into my bed*. We've been inseparable.

The changes he's made to the school are already obvious. Marks have gone up all around. Money has flowed in. There are more resources to share. A better atmosphere. I'm happier and, most importantly, the students are happier.

It's just like it was when I was a student here, and Skipper's done all this.

And I might've helped a *teeny tiny* bit. Turns out I know how to run a good school. Who knows, maybe one day I might make a good principal.

And that's what led me to be back in my classroom, on the night of the reopening of the school, checking out my sexy ass in the sexy dress Skipper's bought me.

"I do look pretty damn sexy," I reply to Skipper as he comes over and rubs up against me. We both look at ourselves in the mirror. He's wearing an expensive tux. We match like two perfect dolls. A perfect couple.

"Think back on all those years ago, when we used to study in this same room," Skipper says, touching my back with his hands. His fingers rub up and down my exposed skin, making me tingle all over. God, I love this man. "Think about all the naughty things we used to do in this classroom."

I laugh. "I'll never forget what you used to do to me in here."

"How about we make some more memories?"

I purr. "Oh, I agree. Let's."

"Hang on one moment," Skipper says, breaking away from me. I groan at his departure from my body. I was really starting to like how I could feel his stiff erection against my ass. "I've got a little surprise for you, Miss Finn."

"What is it?"

Skipper skips over to the classroom door and opens in. Two boys walk in. James and Tom.

What? No way.

They're both dressed in matching tuxedos as well.

My hands raise to my chest at the sight of them together dressed up like this. *So cute.*

"Go ahead, boys," Skipper says.

James and Tom walk right up to me and being speaking in unison. "My bounty is as boundless as the sea, my love as deep; the more I give to thee. The more I have, for both are infinite."

Aw, they're quoting Romeo and Juliet at me.

My favorite play. The one I taught them.

I turn to congratulate Skipper on organizing this cute display, but he's no longer standing.

He's on one knee.

No.

He winks at James, who brings out a little box from behind his back and gives it to me.

No freaking way.

My heart pounds in my chest as I open the box, and inside there's a ring.

"Will you marry me, Miss Finn?" Skipper asks.

This time, I can't hold back my tears.

"Yes," I reply.

And that's the day my Romeo asked me to marry him.

WANT to find out about Cliff's own love story?

Go to rebeccacastle.com to find the links for The Chef (Surfer Town #3)

ABOUT THE AUTHOR

Rebecca has had the storytelling bug since... forever!

What Rebecca likes most is writing steamy hot filthy romances with sweet happy endings sprinkled with some delicious bad boys.

Born and raised in an Aussie coastal town, she loves travelling around the world - meeting new people and discovering their stories.

Aside from adventuring she also enjoys a good rainy day in with a good book or at a hot beach catching the sun.

She's a world-class napping professional. You'll most likely find her asleep snuggled up on a sofa somewhere cozy.

For other titles and information please visit
rebeccacastle.com

facebook.com/rebeccacastleauthor
instagram.com/rebeccacastle.author